T0149190

# Venice BACKSTREETS

## THE YEAR IN THE VENICE PALAZZO

## BLUE LYNN BLAKE

authorHOUSE®

*AuthorHouse™*
*1663 Liberty Drive*
*Bloomington, IN 47403*
*www.authorhouse.com*
*Phone: 1 (800) 839-8640*

*Published by AuthorHouse  12/17/2015*

*ISBN: 978-1-5049-5177-7 (sc)*
*ISBN: 978-1-5049-5178-4 (e)*

*Library of Congress Control Number: 2015915650*

*Print information available on the last page.*

*Any people depicted in stock imagery provided by Thinkstock are models, and such images are being used for illustrative purposes only. Certain stock imagery © Thinkstock.*

*This book is printed on acid-free paper.*

**Venice Backstreets -- The year in the Venice palazzo** is BASED ON a true story. The names have been changed to protect the innocent and the not so innocent.

# CHAPTER ONE

**FOR ONE FABULOUS YEAR,** I lived in a palazzo in Venice. Venice is a total assault on the senses where gypsies squat in the street begging for money next to a jewelry shop window with a $50,000 diamond necklace. Venice is a place where romance, love and survival have endured. And since I was at a point in life that I wanted to endure I came to Venice looking for those things – a beautiful place to live where I could love again.

One year I made a weeklong visit at the end of my year of traveling through Italy. I had been planning to go to Venice ever since I came to Italy the year before, but Venice was such a myth that something held me back from wanting to go there. I didn't want to ruin the romance of dreaming about it. Every time I planned on going there, I put it off. The myth might be ruined by the reality. I went everywhere else -- Rome, Florence, the Lakes, Cinque Terre, the Amafi coast and Sicily. I even spent a month in the remote mountains of Marche on a horse farm. But finally I had to go to Venice before I went home.

I stayed at the convent youth hostel run by an order of nuns near the *Ponte Piccolo* (Little Bridge) on the island of Guidecca. Here, in an old chapel, fifty beds were laid out in four rows under a large portrait of the Crucified Christ. For $12 a night you got a bed, clean sheets and a shower. Girls came from all over the world -- Germany, England, Japan, Canada, Brazil, France, Australia and, of course, America. Like a strict religious school with disciplined rules the nuns kept the international room of girls in order. A nun came in at ten o'clock at night to check to see that everyone was in bed and the lights were turned off. There was no physical way to get in or out of the convent since all the windows were barred. The doors were securely locked and any girl who wanted to come in after ten was left on the street. By nine o'clock in the morning the nuns pushed us out by way of the heavy wooden door so they could have their old convent back until we were let in again at 4:00 o'clock in the afternoon, a line of tired girls stood at the door after a full day of wandering around the streets.

I liked this convent so much that I came back the next summer to spend a month. At night, after we were all locked in by the ten o'clock curfew, I'd sneak into the bathroom and smoke a cigarette by the small barred window while standing on the toilet. There was still that young schoolgirl inside of me wanting to rebel against anything I could find.

But my sojourn at the convent ended when I washed my sheet in the sink. There was a large sign posted in the bathroom -- DO NOT WASH CLOTHES IN THE SINKS – but my sheet was really dirty. The nun came in to check and make sure everyone was in bed and she found the guilty sheet in a bucket on the floor. How she found it I don't know, I had hidden it in the corner of the last toilet stall.

She yelled in English for ten minutes, "Whose sheet is this? I told you, you cannot wash any clothes here. Who did this?"

I, the guilty party, just stuck my head under my pillow as she walked up and down the aisle yelling and looking for the bad girl who committed this horrible crime. There was no way I was going to confess. She would have thrown me out on the street that night. So the next day, seeing my sheet on the line but not daring to go to take it down, I left the convent. Buying a new sheet was a lot better than being yelled at by a nun. I know, I went to Catholic school.

The next year I made another trip back to Venice. My first Italian boyfriend, who I met while living in Assisi, was from Venice. His family moved to Mestre when he was six years old so he doesn't know the city well but he loves it and says with pride that he is Venetian. All Italians are proud, but it seems that Venetians' hold their head higher than anyone else. To be from Venice is to be from a magical island. My boyfriend and I camped on the mainland in Mestre and at sunset we looked across the lagoon at Venice. During the day we took the bus to Venice and wandered around the streets in San Polo to look for his old house. But he couldn't find it. Maybe it was this street or maybe down that street. Even Venetians get lost in Venice.

Two years later I was again in Venice when I went into a week's exile from my married lover who I lived with in Monte Carlo. I went to Venice by myself to give him time to think about whether he was going to ask his wife for a divorce. While I was living with him in his beautiful villa overlooking the Mediterranean Sea, his wife lived in an apartment ten minutes away with her two children from a previous marriage. Their living apart was an arrangement they made before I ever came into the picture. I had lived next to my lover's wife in her apartment building with my Italian boyfriend. I became a nanny to her children and took care of them after their school until she got home from work. The habit of the husband was to stay at home in his villa. He didn't want to be around the children. But he started to come by the apartment for an hour or two before his wife came home at eight. I'd make dinner for him and the children. He liked me making him dinner. I think he liked someone taking care of him. About a month later I started an affair with the husband. This had been going on for two months when I went on a two week motorcycle vacation with the husband through France and Switzerland. During this trip I decided I loved him. He was everything

I ever wanted in a man – sophisticated, charming, well-educated and I was hooked. I came back to live with him in his villa in Monte Carlo and after a month I gave him the ultimatum -- me or his wife. In true French style he would have preferred to keep both of us. I fled to Venice on the night train and took up my residence at the convent hostel. I always felt safe with the nuns. Every day I talked to my lover on the phone, passing each day walking the streets until the afternoon when I could call him not knowing where I would be living a month.

He joined me a week later in Venice. He took the night train from Monte Carlo to Venice, part of the Orient Express. I went to the Santa Lucia train station an hour before his train was scheduled to arrive. His train was late by fifteen minutes. I ran down the train tracks looking for him, searching the faces of the crowd for that smile that would light me up. Expecting him. Not finding him. The quick burst of people rushing from the train were quickly gone. The platform was empty. Still I stayed there waiting. Did he decide not to come? Was everything over? My heart was racing with disappointment and then heighten to ecstatic joy when I saw his face. He casually stepped off the train as if he had all the time in the world. He was a very calculating man. I ran to him, like some forgotten scene from a black and white foreign movie and smothered him in kisses. I swear that everything turned black and white as I ran to greet him. He brushed my hair aside and held me close to his chest as he kissed my forehead.

"I love you and never want to leave you again," he said to me.

The next three days we danced in San Marco square while the moon and the stars looked at us. We took the vaporetto out to Burano holding each other close and tight with my head on his shoulder. We walked along the beach at Lido and took two chairs at the Hotel du Bain on the beach. We got stinking drunk at the Chioggia bar across from Palazzo Ducale while listening to jazz, ordering drink after drink until they closed the bar and we stumbled quietly back to our hotel room. But mostly we fought. We yelled so much while sitting at a table in the street on *Calle Figher* that the very proper English couple next to us got up and left.

Of course I was yelling things like, "If you think I'm going to be your fucking mistress while you stay married to your wife, you're crazy. No American girl would do anything like that."

No, American girls have morals. Yes we do. Well, we usually do. Well, we like to think we do.

So this story is about a regular American girl who goes to Venice and does some, well, not very American middle-class things.

# CHAPTER TWO

VENICE is fairytale. The city is real, but its name is a myth – an imagined world of novels, movies and paintings. It is a quick stop on a tour or a place where a movie is filmed or a painting on the wall. The city seems so dark and full of shadows at night and so bright and glaring during the day. It's as though you could never get a really good look at the city. She, for Venice could be nothing but a woman, seems unknowable. She is two-faced, always changing, a chaste nun and a painted whore.

I made my last trip to Venice was when I was escaping from America again. After my disastrous affair with the lover from Monte Carlo I went back to America. I could barely do anything else. The day I left my French lover's villa my legs were shaking so much I could barely walk down the stairs. I was scared to death thinking I had barely escaped the day with my life. He would tell me in detail how he planned to kill me. His love/hatred feelings for America somehow got combined with his feeling for me. I believed he would murder me one day if I stayed.

So I went back to California and tried to return to the life I once had. But I wasn't the same person. I had lunch with my old girlfriends and they listened and marveled at my life in Europe but they never called me again. I was no longer a regular American girl. I couldn't get a job either. Not even as a sales clerk and I had once owned two stores. So for two years I just tried to get up in the morning and get some exercise. It was two years I was really dead inside. I couldn't find a new life in L.A. Or anywhere in America. I had to do something, but what? Finally I decided to move back to Italy. I had no idea where I would live but I prayed Italy would revive me. That I would find some reason to live again. I was that close to not wanting to live at all.

It was February when I arrived at the airport in Rome. When you decide to change your life you cannot think about too many things at once. One day at a time. My only thought on the airplane was to get a hotel room. I'd been to Rome several times and knew the area by the train station. After I got the hotel room then I would think about where I would go, where I would live and what my future would be. But the first thing to do in Rome was to get a bed and some sleep. Then I would decide where I would go. Where my new home would be?

Would I go back to Assisi or Cortona? Or the lakes? Or maybe Florence? There are so many choices. I didn't even think of Venice because the last time I was there it was with my Monte Carlo lover. I didn't want to go anywhere that reminded me of him.

In February it was freezing in Rome. The thought of going north didn't appeal to me. After four days in Rome I went south. As far south as you can go and still be in Italy -- Sicily. I stayed in another convent (bless those nuns) for a month in Noto on the southern coast of Sicily near Syracuse. I watched the cherry trees bloom with the spring flowers and thought I needed to bloom again. I needed to find somewhere where I could flourish. My long winter of regret and depression was over. It was time to move on. After a month of walking the streets of Noto, I still had no idea where to go when I got to the train station in Syracuse. I looked at the train schedule posted on the wall. On the schedule was a train that began in Syracuse went overnight and the next day up the Italian peninsula and ended in Venice. That was my train. I would go to Venice. I would live in Venice.

I shared my sleeping compartment with two Italian women. One was on her way to Campaigna and the other to Bologna. They were home visiting their families in Sicily but they worked in northern Italy. The north is where the money is and the jobs are, southern Italy is still poor, still hanging on to the old traditions, still living in another century. I sat in that train seat looking at the Italian towns as we rolled up the Italian peninsula. After twenty hours on the train I looked out the window to see

Venice sitting magically on the water. My city. The city that would become my city. That view reminded me of the movie *Summertime* with Katherine Hepburn when she first arrived in Venice on the train. The only difference is that Katherine Hepburn arrived in the summer. When I arrived in Venice it was the first day of March. A foot of snow covered the town of Venice.

So I was finally back in Venice. Again. It wasn't the Venice I had known all those times before in the summer. It was cold and snowing but still incredibly beautiful. The moment you walk down the steps of the train station you know you are somewhere special, somewhere like no other city in the world. Venice is a place of dreams, set apart on an island, so near to reality but set in its own time. As you walk out of the train station the Grand Canal sweeps before you with ancient churches and palaces as a backdrop. The boats whiz by, people climb the bridge to cross to the other side of the canal. It is crazy. Wonderful, beautiful crazy. You are immediately drawn into this magical world and its confusing life.

I took the vaporetto to *Casa d' Oro* (House of Gold) and dragged my suitcase through the snow trying to find a room for the night. In my Venice Tourist Guide I had spotted a hotel, the cheapest on the list, which was on a street behind the *Strada Nova* (The New Street) near the d'Oro vaporetto stop. But the streets are complicated. Short alleys that end at a canal. Mazes of streets with a strange combination of numbers. House numbers are not in order. In the bleak coldness of the afternoon all the houses looked uninviting and many of the houses looked like no one has lived there for years. The directions given to me by the hotel's receptionist were impossible to follow. I had come to Venice to find myself and I was lost. I had come to find my life in the sun and I was freezing in the snow. It took a half an hour to find the hotel which was only five minutes from the vaporetto stop.

Finally seeing the little sign of the hotel on a side street I had found my refuge. I told the receptionist that I wanted a single and I planned to stay a month and I was willing to pay twenty Euro a night for a room that had the printed price of thirty Euro. It was the middle of winter, the carnavale was over, and the season wouldn't pick up for two more months. He accepted my offer. So I had a home. For a month anyway.

My room was basically a closet with a single bed with a small barred window looking out on a back alley filled with trash. So what if I wasn't staying at the Ritz. I was in Venice. I was finally in Venice again and this time I meant to make it my home. Never did I dream I would end up living in his beautiful city of Venice, not in all the times I visited it before. I was raised in Florida. I went to Catholic school, worked at McDonalds, graduated from college, bought a car, got a good job, bought a house, got married, open my own store ... but none of these things made me really happy. It seemed like I was just living out a script that society had decided for me. I really was feeling suppressed and I was looking for my real life. All my life I did what I was supposed to do. I did what was expected from me. But I was unfulfilled. There must be something more than living in a 4 bedroom, 3 bath house with a swimming pool and driving a car for an hour to work every day.

My life's goals were to make other people happy. First of all, I had to make myself someone my mother would be proud of. I was a difficult teenager (on a scale from 1 to 10, I was a 7) and I felt I had to make it up to her. My whole family thought of me as the problem child. I did finally graduate from college and got a great job in the computer industry in Minnesota. Everything was set for my future. I bought a house and planted tulips and opened a 401K. Then I got married moved to California and was trying to please my husband by being the perfect wife and business woman (i.e. making a lot of money). We bought a big house (for our future kids) with the required swimming pool and a second home in Tahoe. Again I was set. But when my husband and I moved to Santa Barbara we got divorced and I opened a decorating store. My life was again set being a perfect girlfriend to my wayward boyfriend and the perfect interior designer for all my customers. A lot of my ambition was just trying to become good enough for them to love me. If I made a lot of money, they (whoever they were at the moment – my mother, my sister, my boyfriend, my friends) would finally really love me or so I thought. I would become good enough, pretty enough, rich enough to love. But playing the American game just the way it was supposed to be played wasn't enough. Just making more money and buying more things wasn't enough. It wasn't what I wanted. The life I was living in America wasn't the life I wanted to live. I didn't want to spend my life in a car commuting on the 101 freeway. Driving forever down the endless highways of Minneapolis or San Francisco or Los Angeles. I didn't want a boyfriend who was cheating on me. Who was asking me for money then leaving to go who knows where. I hated that choking feeling in my throat. So I changed my life. I left my boyfriend, sold my business, sold or gave away everything I owned. And I just left. Some things were hard to give away like my Blue Willow china from my great grandmother or my Japanese china which my mother gave me, but, well, I don't just want to be my possessions. I want to be my dreams. So Part One was -- figure out what your dreams are. And where better to figure out your dreams than in Italy.

There was nothing in my up keeping to predict that I would someday live in Venice except, if I admit it, even as a girl I dreamed of the life. Well, I dreamed of living in a foreign land, sleeping in a beautiful palace, of making love to a handsome man (or men as the case may be), of being free, of wearing beautiful clothes. Of wearing diamonds and walking around in pretty, charming shoes. Of having fresh flowers in my bedroom. I dreamed of having full control over my life. Of living without restraint. So I came to live in Venice, a city with no restraints and plenty of opportunities.

# CHAPTER THREE

**VENICE** was a chance for a new life. I couldn't find anything in myself to build on when I went back to live in America. As Scarlet once said, 'nothing to live for, nothing to fight for.' Venice would revived me. It was a chance to live again. The moment I stepped out into the streets of Venice I felt hopeful for the first time in years. Like maybe there was a future for me. A good future. A hopeful future.

After settling into my little room I walked through the snow to *San Marco Square*. No one was in the square and at four-thirty the sun was already setting into the lagoon. Across from the *Ducale Palace* I went to the *Chioggia Bar* with a view of the square and the lagoon with the snow covered gondolas. The last time I was in this bar was when I was drunk with my old lover. In the empty café

I settled down at a table with a pot of tea and tucked myself into a chair to contemplate my new life.

Venice is an island city surrounded by water. A city of little islands in a lagoon protected from the open sea by the long, narrow island of Lido. A hundred fingers of water drift through the city and as the water floats by it sweeps you up along with it and all your dreams seem like they might possibly come true.

Venice is a city of beautiful colors -- pale rose stones, alabaster marble, graying wood painted in all the hues of yellow, peach, gold, scarlet and pink. Hundreds of years of paint fading into new colors which we try to reproduce in America – Sienna Red or Sorrento Lemon Yellow. Then there is the sea and the sky, all blue -- various colors of blue. In the west the snow-capped Dolomite Mountains promise to keep your dream safe from the outside world. Protected by the mountains and the sea, I would step on to a stage and the play of my life would begin. Again. Another act. Hopefully this act would have a happy ending.

To understand Venice you must know about her history. She was one of the major powers in Europe for a thousand years. Venice was the first republic in her time and in the 15th century was as powerful as France or England or the Holy Roman Empire. All the goods from China, Arabia and India were funneled through Venice to Europe. It was a city of immense riches. It was the city of money. The renaissance city of money. A city where money was made and where money was spent. It's said that one dollar invested in a ship from Venice to the Orient brought back a thousand dollars in return. Can you imagine what Wall Street would be like with odds like that? The palaces that line the streets by the hundreds were built by those rich men. And rich men want the best. Even in Shakespeare's time it was a dream -- a setting for a very nice play about a merchant.

After America was discovered, the world changed and Venice was no longer the center of the world. The rich merchants became hosts to European tourists. After the French Revolution, Napoleon's armies stretched its arms into Venice. Napoleon came. Lord Byron came. Then Mussolini came. Hitler came too. Even Brad and Angie came. And George got married there. Yes, Venice is a city that is eternally famous where even the famous come for validation and to show that they have arrived.

Venice has two famous sons, famous for centuries throughout the world. Even as a child I knew these two names --Marco Polo and Casanova. As a child I played Marco Polo in the swimming pool in my back yard and knew about this adventurer who traveled to China and the court of Genghis Khan. As a frisky teenager I read Casanova's autobiography. But never did I dream I would end up living in Venice. But I guess if I could have two patron saints it would be these two men -- one known as a great adventurer and the other as a great lover.

The first week in Venice I carefully avoided San Marco Square after my night in the snow covered square. The square had too many memories for me. And for a woman alone it is a hunting ground and she is the prey. San Marco square is the place where men scout for women. It has been like this for hundreds of years. Men, in groups of two or three, would meet and rate the girls in the square. They were looking for prey. The men in Venice have jobs but there real work is picking up girls. It's their life's work and ambition. Their tradition. Their duty. Some liked young girls but others preferred an older woman who was easier to pick up. If other cultures like young girls, the Italians tend to rule them out. Perhaps it's because the younger girls are still living with their mothers. Marriage, marriage, marriage is all the young girls talk about while being watched by their hawk-like mothers. The women in Venice are watched closely by their families. Sex with a Venetian woman is very complicated. There are too many expectations. Too many eyes. Too many mouths. The Venetian men may marry the local women but it's the foreign tourists they have sex with.

The preferred prey is any English speaking girl -- American, English, Canadian or Australian. They are here for adventure (remember Katharine Hepburn in *Summertime*) and an affair with a handsome Italian man is usually on the itinerary, preferably just after the tour of San Marco church and before dinner on the Grand Canal. They are usually on a schedule -- two days here, one day there. A quick and efficient affair. The traveling girl doesn't have that much time to say no. And the great thing about these girls is they have a life, a good job wherever they come from. Any girl from one of these countries spent a lot of money to get to Venice. They might dream of staying in Italy, of living in a palazzo on the Grand Canal but when they wake up they're not really interested in staying. They have their own life to get back to at home. After a quick affair they're gone, like a pleasant day on the beach, appreciated while it is here but soon forgotten and replaced by another beautiful day.

The second preference is any girl from the former communist countries. These girls, many who are very beautiful, are willing to have sex but they often put a price tag -- marriage or at least the promise of marriage -- is part of the bargain. They might not ask for it at the beginning but for them living in Italy is a lot better than living from wherever they came from, so even a not so attractive Italian man can have a very pretty and young girlfriend. An Italian man, who is a friend of mine, got caught up in such a problem. He met a very pretty and much younger girl from Russia. He was married but after two years the girl wanted to get married. His wife found out, he got divorced, the girl found someone else. End of story -- except now he is alone and miserable. It's not always such a perfect life for Venetian men.

"They are cold," a male friend of mine says about the old Communist country girls. Well, can you blame them, they came from repressed and cold cultures. We are luckier in America, luckier than we can imagine. We are the most free females who have ever lived any place or any time on earth.

The thing I like best about Italian men is that they like older women. In America it's still unusual for a younger man and an older woman to be together no matter how many programs about cougars there are on television. Except if you're a movie star. Even then he might not stay forever. But in Italy, men do prefer an older woman.

Someone who can teach them. They all have seen porno films but now they want someone to practice with. And an older woman will show them the ropes (sometimes literally show them the ropes). Many Italian men learn about sex from an older woman and often a lot older -- say twenty or thirty years older. An older woman will teach him what to do and will do many things a young girl would never do. Before moving to Venice I had never been in Venice alone, without a boyfriend, but now that I was alone I was a bit wary of the men. I would leave San Marco Square alone for the time being. I was looking for more than a quick affair.

Every day I took a walk to the far end of Venice to the park in *Santa Elena* called the Pineta (Pine Tree). This little patch of pine trees and grass is unique in Venice, a city that has been stacked with houses for centuries. Here it's a little bit of the countryside in Venice. I'd sit on the bench looking back toward Venice and the bell tower in the square. There are many squares in Venice, but only one 'The Square' -- *San Marco Square*. I was sitting on the bench when a well-dressed man asked me in Italian if I was visiting Venice. He was a doctor and lived nearby. Everything seemed so easy in Venice, the first day you are in Venice you're just sitting on a bench when a nice-looking doctor comes by and asks you for a date. We met that evening in San Marco Square. He took me for a pizza near my hotel. But I hesitated about doing anything with him. He was pleasant and nice but I went back to my hotel room instead of going back to his apartment. I wasn't ready yet. I needed the city to myself for a while.

# CHAPTER FOUR

AFTER two weeks in Venice I started to look for an apartment. I was sure I would get some work here and I did have enough money for one year even if I didn't get a job. Walking by the *Rialto Bridge* one day I saw an apartment advertised in the window of a realtor's office. It was a palace. It was a palace with frescos on the wall and a Murano chandelier in the salon. Looking at the picture, I dreamed a little, then walked on. I should not be looking at a beautiful apartment in a palazzo. The price was high, a thousand Euro a month. Most apartments in Venice are around seven hundred to eight hundred and fifty Euro, some studios you could get for five hundred. I did have the money from America, but shouldn't I be conservative? Get something simple. There was another place for five hundred Euro posted in the window, a single room with a kitchen in a closet. I made myself forget about the palazzo and made an appointment to see the little, cheap apartment.

It was a small apartment with a narrow staircase on the fourth floor not far from the Arsenale. That was in the boondocks as far as Venice was concerned.

That night I went back to the real estate office's window and looked at the pictures of the palazzo again. I was crazy to think about living in such a place. But it would be fantastic. Could I really live in a beautiful palace in Venice? It was a dream of a lifetime.

I went to sleep thinking about that apartment. I woke up thinking about that apartment. I did have enough money to live in that apartment for a year even if I never got a job. Boldly I made an appointment to look at it. Looking wouldn't hurt. I was just looking, I told myself.

Following the young agent from the real estate office I walked to the *Fondemente della Misirecordia*, which is a street in Cannaregio with palazzos on one side and a small canal on the other. The entrance to the building was a large grand hallway, not for living but just for walking through, in the old days this space was for horses and storage. Nothing of value was left on the ground floor because it usually floods at least once a year in Venice. At the end of the hall was an indoor well complete with cupids playing in the plaster. The stairs to the upper floors were wide and grand. The agent introduced me to the owner, an older man, impeccably dressed at ten o'clock in the morning in a suit despite the fact he no longer worked. I love the men in Venice for this reason – they are always well dressed. He kissed my hand. He opened the door to the apartment. It was a large living room, about thirty feet wide with twenty foot high ceilings. Frescos of angels in white floated over the marble fireplace and the doors. It was furnished with modern sofas and dining room table and hutch for the china. A large chandelier from Murano dominated the room. The kitchen was small and modern. The bathroom was grand with a large bathtub, toilet, bidet and sink and a cupboard for towels. The bedroom was enormous. It was another large room the same size as the living room with the tall ceilings and another Murano chandelier over the bed. Two windows looked out over the street of *Fondementa della Misericordia* and the canal that ran next to it. Everything was supplied from the linen and towels to the plates, silverware and pots and pans in the kitchen. There was no question in my mind. Two weeks later I was in my new home.

My apartment in Venice was in a palazzo, a palace, built in the 15th century. Its stone walls stood for five hundred years across the canal from the convent of *Santa Maria di Servi*. It had seen the doges of Venice rule and die out. It had seen Napoleon's French soldiers and Hitler's German soldiers walk along the streets. It had even seen the American GI's who liberated the city after World War II. The apartment was on the third floor of the four floor building and was owned by my eighty-year-old landlord. He was a gentleman in every sense of the word. He kissed my hand every time he saw me. The building had been divided by his grandfather between different cousins, each cousin getting a full floor with three apartments. He lived with his gracious wife in one apartment in the back which looked over the canal *Rio della Sensa*. His daughter and her son lived in the apartment next to mine. I had the grand apartment, the one with frescos and bedroom windows which looked out over the canal and the convent. The apartment was an exorbitant price by Venetian terms. A thousand Euro a month, only a foreigner would pay that. In Los Angeles or Miami or Hawaii, I would get a cramped studio apartment for that amount of money. I happily paid that amount and thought myself the luckiest girl in the world.

Moving in was one of the happiest days of my life. I deposited my two suitcases in the bedroom and began to investigate my new home.

The living room faced an inner courtyard where two windows on either side of the fireplace looked out to the other apartments in the building. The best part of the apartment were the frescos painted on the walls -- little cherubs, against a background of pale green, who held ribbons while flying across my walls as they had done for hundreds of years. They smiled at me as they would every day. These *putti*, from the Italian word for little boy, were naked chubby babies and became my roommates in the palazzo.

I opened the windows in the bedroom and watched the people walking up and down the street. Small boats whizzed by in the canal. A boat carrying vegetables stopped below my window. There was a small vegetable market on the street level below my window. A strong, young good-looking man got out of the boat and carried the vegetables to the store. (I should say just one thing right now which will save me from repeating myself. All the young Italian men are good-looking. There's something right with those Italian genes. If you are a woman, this is a good place to admire men.) Later I would shop in this vegetable market which was owned by an older man and his two sons.

From my window I could easily see the walled-in yard of the convent of *Santa Maria di Servi*. The convent was now a primary school and a dormitory for students attending the *University of Venice*. In the summer it was a hostel. I watched the little kids play on the jungle gym and laugh on the swings. The stone wall by the canal had some obvious patches. These were made perhaps by the nuns who would escape the nunnery during the night to meet their lovers. Hundreds of years ago many Venetian women were sent to nunneries because their families couldn't afford the dowry needed for a good marriage. In those days a woman had three and only three choices in life -- a wife, a nun or a whore. Hopefully I would have a few more choices. Actually, my choice would be to be all three in one. I was in heaven. I found my place in the world. Now in my apartment, I was ready for my next task. I would look for work and more importantly for love.

# CHAPTER FIVE

EVEN after I moved into my palazzo, I never went to San Marco Square at night. It was too predatory. I had the strong feeling of being one of those ducks in a shooting gallery. In my previous visits to Venice I went to San Marco Square every evening. I would sit and order a $10 Coca-Cola around seven o'clock and watch the people and listen to the music from the live orchestras while the sun set. I always went to the same café in the square and I always had the same beautiful waiter. Alright, I went there because of the waiter. After three nights I stayed a little later than normal and went back to the bathroom. When I came out my waiter was waiting for me. He took me by the hand and led me outside to the dark corridor that ran behind the building. There, against a damp cold wall, we made out for five minutes. He asked me if he could come to my room. I was staying at the convent, so that was out of the question, so I never saw the waiter again. It had been years since that happened but I walked by the bar to see if he still worked there, but he was gone. It's a good thing that memories do not fade as quickly as people fade out of your life. I consoled myself by remembering he was married with three kids in Mestre.

One morning I walked by one of the glass factories not far from San Marco Square. A young man followed me down the street and placed himself in front of me. He was short but very muscular with dark hair. His face was like a dark Italian Gregory Peck. Not a bad combination.

"I saw you walking by," he said in broken English, "and I cannot let such a beauty just walk by without talking to her."

He did not look too comfortable with himself but he held his head high as if looking courageous might give him courage.

I looked at him without speaking. It was his boldness despite his shyness that made me friendly toward him. I didn't say anything to him but I didn't walk on.

"I came running after you. You are so beautiful," he said in his heavily accented English, "My boss will be angry but I don't care."

Normally, I would not have given him the time of day. I had been approached hundreds of times on the streets of Venice since I arrived. Not that I'm beautiful. In fact, it's the not the really beautiful girls that the men go after here. They know their chances of success are better with the girls who are just average. Since I had been in Venice I'd been in a self-imposed convent of my single room at the hotel. Now that I had my beautiful apartment, I guess it was time to take another leap. And this young man was the one to do it with.

"Here is my number," I said giving him a card from the ones I had printed which I had intended to use to find some English students.

"I see you tonight," he said as he took the card, smiled and fled. I fled in the opposite direction. Oh well, here I go again. Isn't life fun.

He called me five minutes later.

"I wanted to see if this is really your number," he said.

"Yes, of course it is."

Does he think I get cards made up with my name and fake number? Well maybe that wouldn't be such a bad idea. He re-made our date for that night.

I waited for him in my boudoir (I think boudoir is the proper name for my Venetian bedroom). I saw him walking down the street with short confident steps. He was going to get laid tonight -- every muscle in his body yelled out. He came up to my apartment with a bottle of wine. We both knew why he was at my apartment and we quickly got down to business. We took a sip of the wine after I poured it and didn't take another sip until after we were finished. It was only after the second sip of wine when I found out his name -- Mario.

His hands were strong as he pulled my body next to his, his lips soft as he kissed my back and his tongue was forceful as he kissed my mouth. His passion was boiling. Italian men take their roles as lovers very seriously. The worst thing you can say to a man is that he is a lousy lover. Nothing will offend him more. So, I can say Mario was a good lover. He was a very good lover indeed.

The next day I went to the park and felt like I was in love. Venice does that to you or Italy does it to you. It's just really easy to feel like you're in love here. I was in the park in Sant'Elena which gives two great views – looking east there is the island of Lido with the scattering of small islands and toward the west there is the city of downtown Venice (downtown being San Marco Square) with, on very clear days, the Dolomite mountains in the background.

Yes, I definitely feel in love looking at that view. Mario was younger than me. How much younger I don't know but definitely younger. I remembered his hard muscled body as he pressed against mine the night before. I have dated a few younger men in California before, the youngest was ten years younger but I have never felt comfortable in that situation. I prefer dating older men and now I fear any younger man I am with is looking at my flaws. I try not to smile because when I do smile my eyes are surrounded by a mess of wrinkles. But it's really hard not to smile when you're in Venice and when you're in love. So I grinned. Just like the cat who ate the mouse.

I laid down in the grass and gaze up at the pine trees. Yes, this will be nice, I imagined, Mario and me. We'll live in my beautiful palazzo and come to this park and eat a delicious picnic dinner that I've prepared as we watch the sun go down. As I am lying down with my fantasy about Mario, a man comes up to me.

"Ciao," he said but I can tell by his accent he's not Italian.

"No, no," I responded seriously. I did not want anyone to disturb my dream of Mario and the night before.

"I'm from Greece," he told me.

Yea, yea I think to myself and turned over. "No thank you," I mumble to myself, "I've already found Mr. Right."

I waited anxiously for Mario to call me that night. He didn't call. So he's playing that game, I thought to myself. Well I won't call him either. For a week this went on -- no calls. Finally, after seven days he called me.

"I want to meet you tonight."

My sister had arrived for a visit a few days before. Meeting Mario at my apartment was now impossible.

"My sister's here. You can't come to my apartment," I told him as an excuse why I couldn't see him at all.

"Ok", he said without hesitation. "Meet me by the Rialto market at nine. And wear high-heels."

High-heels in Venice!

Let's take a moment and review the situation about high-heels in Venice. The entire city is made up of cobblestone streets and countless bridges. Wearing high-heels in Venice is about as practical as wearing high-heels in the sand. You're just not going to get anywhere fast.

But ... Venice is renowned for her shoes and in particular high-heeled shoes. Five hundred years ago the Venetian women where wobbling around on eight inch heels and often needed two servants to help them walk. So there's a long standing tradition with the high-heeled foot and sex. And the shoes in Venice. I'm not a shoe person. I'm practical in my flats but I can spend hours and hours looking and adoring the pieces of art they have in the shoe stores in Venice. The Italians take producing a pair of shoes very seriously. It is an art form. And it is a form of seduction. In Venice there are two shops that will even make you a custom, unique, one-of-a-kind shoe for you so magical that you will believe little fairies made them.

But practical? So I put on a pair of high-heels in my purse and I wore my flats for the walk to the Rialto.

"I'm going out for a little bit," I told my sister and disappeared into the night. Before I crossed the Rialto Bridge I changed my flats for my four inch black heels. OMG, my feet hurt already and I haven't even taken a step. I walked slowly. Slow is sexy anyway. In the now deserted marketplace of the fruit and vegetable market I saw Mario. My blood was rushing through my body and landing right between my legs. The minute I put my hands on his hard body I was ready. So he didn't call me for a week, all is forgiven. He took my hand and led me back to a back streets in-between the canal and San Polo square. He knew a little courtyard and pushed me against the wall to kiss me. A cat meowed in the alleyway. Mario turned me around so my face was pressed against the wall. He kissed my neck then twisted my head to kiss my mouth. He knelt down and pulled my underwear down. He kissed my ass as I pushed my face against the cold hard wall. Heat and cold together. That's Venice. The cat's meowing kept me on earth. But his kisses were soft and wet. I felt myself floating into timeless pleasure.

Oh, yea, Venice *IS* nice.

We heard someone walking toward us. Mario got up and kissed me against the wall as a man walked by.

Back to earth.

"Andiamo," he said to me. "Let's go".

"Dove?" I asked him. "Where?"

"A casa."

His house.

Just two blocks away he unlocked a large door but not before looking both ways to see if anyone in the street was watching us.

"Sssh," he said to me and took me by the hand up a maze of staircases. He did not turn on the light. Another key opened the door to the apartment. A light in the hallway was on. Mario left me at the door then disappeared for a minute into the darkness of the apartment.

"Good, no one is home," he says to me when he returns.

The entrance led to a small kitchen, not updated since the 1930's. Beyond the kitchen was an extremely large living room about thirty feet wide by fifty feet long. There were boxes of china and books everywhere. The room was filled with mismatched sofas, chairs, lamps, and tables, not arranged in any order but stacked together like some small furniture store with too much furniture. Mario explained his family was selling the apartment and they were moving things. There must have been hundreds of years of things in that apartment.

"Why are you moving?" I asked.

"Too expensive. To heat this apartment costs over eight hundred Euro a month."

"Who lives here?"

"Me and my father and my brother."

"And your mother?"

"She's dead a long time."

Through the living room we walked until we got to a very small room with a single bed. It was Mario's bedroom. He stripped me of my dress and threw it on the floor. He quickly yet carefully took off his own clothes. As I laid naked in bed he neatly placed his clothes over a chair.

I got on my hands and knees and looked out the beautiful Venetian glass windows to the streetlight below.

Two hours later Mario escorted me down the stairway to the street. It was midnight and I walked home by myself.

I had asked Mario why it took so long so him to call me back. He said his father was sick and he needed to stay with him. Appeased by his explanation, I waited for Mario's next phone call.

He never did call.

In order to save the reader the long agony of the next few weeks or myself the need to remember it in any detail, all I will say is that Mario never called me and I was pissed and dejected and Italy wasn't supposed to be like this. I was supposed to fall in love. Venice is a city of love. The city of romance. Getting fucked and dropped isn't romantic.

If men ever wonder why women bite their heads off when all they say is a simple "Hi" it is because of her last relationship. Women like to stew and her last boyfriend's words, actions and deeds will brew until she boils over and yells at some other guy. They're all the same, aren't they? OK, maybe they're not all the same but it's sure convenient to think so.

One night, about a month after my date with Mario, I was walking in San Marco square alone and I admit I was looking for Mario. My sister was still visiting me but I had left her at home after our dinner and gone out on my own. In between my anger of being dropped by Mario, I was taking a brief moment to actually listen to one of the orchestras in the square.

"Raindrops on roses and whiskers on kittens," was being played by the orchestra at the Austrian bar. Now who can be mad when they are playing that?

"We both are wearing white," I heard a voice behind me say.

I turned around and saw a very good looking man. He had brownish blond hair, brown eyes and a neatly manicured goatee. His face looked like something out of a French movie about medieval soldiers. He was, indeed, all in white. A white knight perhaps? We women are undying romantics. Damn Cinderella and her Prince.

The man wore a white cotton shirt opened to below his chest. White cotton pants. Rings on his fingers. Several bracelets on his wrist. And a necklace.

You've got to be kidding me, I thought to myself. Is this guy for real? He looks like an ad for an Italian gigolo.

"Would you like to have a drink?" he asked me.

I looked at him up and down and hesitated. Another Casanova I thought to myself. I had just been with a Casanova and wasn't really interested in another. Besides he looked a little too skinny for my taste. I prefer the big muscles. But I was mad at Mario and that was all it took to say yes to him.

The moment I walked off with this man I knew he was a perfect player. He had perfected picking up women, the way an architect would perfect a building or an artist would perfect his painting style. It was an art form. He had a system that included a timetable based on how long a girl was in town. For the one nighters he would speed up the process. For someone like me who lived in Venice (his least favorite conquest because that could mean complications later on) he would take his time. In the square, his hunting ground, he was in pursuit of his prey. A true hunter. Now that the prey was caught, he would take his time playing with it before devouring it.

He was handsome, articulate, charming and enthusiastic. He was mostly enthusiastic about Venice and as we walked toward the bar he paused to tell me the story of the bell tower and the horses on San Marco Church.

"Welcome to Venice," he said as though he was a tourist guide. "The republic of Venice began in 868. For a thousand years we were a republic and the Venetians ruled the Mediterranean Sea and all the booty that came from India and China to Europe went through Venice. It was a boom town for hundreds of years and many fortunes were made and palaces were built. Venice is a city of palaces, although many are today run down, there are still plenty of Murano chandeliers hanging from the ceilings. This town was made on money and today it still has the finest things that money can buy -- shoes, jewelry, clothes and, of course, women. Venice was and is still known for its beautiful women, the courtesans."

"Courtesans?" I asked.

"Courtesans were very important to the city. The courtesans brought love and romance to the city and men would come from all over Europe to enjoy the attentions of Venice's courtesans. They were the most beautiful women in all the world."

"You mean whores," I said not wanting to be swept away by his tales of tail.

"No, a courtesan was not a whore. She was an educated woman and a woman of culture. She offered a man sex, that's true, but she also offered him amusing companionship. A whore is simply a quick fuck and can be gotten on any street corner."

"And what qualities would you say a courtesan had?" I asked.

"As for your question," he answered me, "I guess a Courtesan would be good looking, very sexy with proper seducing clothes and hot but always with nice manners and beautiful movements like for instance when she brought food to her mouth she would caress it and eat in slowly as though she was devouring not the food but a man's cock. Or perhaps she touches herself when looking at a man. She also has to behave as though she really loves her dates. Prostitutes are always so detached from their clients. Of course class and education can definitely make the difference too. You have got these qualities. You would make a very good courtesan."

"You don't even know me," I said.

*Who was this guy anyway telling me about courtesans? What was he -- on a recruiting team?*

"No, I don't know you. But all women want to be courtesans."

"Oh really," I said.

*There was no point even discussing the matter. How could any man make such a stupid statement?*

We walked by the canal near Harry's Bar. An hour ago I was on this bridge trying to call Mario and now I was with this man. All those little canals running through the city and gondoliers singing in the middle of a lagoon had its intended effect. I was already starting to fall under this man's spell.

As though reading my mind he said to me, "Venice is a very romantic city. A city for love."

When he said the word love the only thing I could think of is the only thing this man loved is himself. But, well when in Rome ...

I could play the love game as well as any man.

We went to have a quick drink standing up at the bar (because in Italy you pay about a third of the price if you stand up at the bar instead of sitting down). I guess he wasn't ready to fork over a large amount of money unless he could be assured he'd get something out of it. We talked a little but he was more interested in telling me about Venice than in knowing anything about me. He looked around the bar to see who was around and to see who was looking at him and his newest conquest. He nodded to a few people. He looked satisfied with himself. Ripe from Mario's rejection I was looking good that night and was flirting with my eyes with every man in the bar. I wanted to feel some power of being a woman. When I went up stairs to the bathroom the waiter followed me (another waiter and another bar on the square. Was this was becoming a ritual?) As I stood in front of the sink I slowly put on my red lipstick giving the waiter a look like I'd like to do something else with my lips to him. But I quickly ran down the stairs to my gigolo before anything could happen with my new flirt. (Despite all the evidence in this book to the contrary, I am sometimes a chicken and can easily lose my nerve).

My guide, restless to show off his prey, took me to a table between the café across from the Palazzo Ducale and the park facing the lagoon and the island of Guidecca. This cafe wasn't open at night so anyone could sit at the tables for free. Actually, it's a really great spot, quieter than the square and there is always a moon and a row of gondolas on the waters of the lagoon to stare at.

We sat down at the table and I asked him his name.

"Raphael," he said.

Raphael, I thought, it figures. He looks like someone out of a painting. I was always stuck by the faces of Italian men. They are so pure -- so purely delicious. It only took a few minutes and I was no longer thinking of Mario. Who's Mario? -- *I bet you forgot about him too.*

I asked Raphael where he worked. He worked at the same glass factory store as Mario. *Oh great, do all the studs in Venice work at that store. They work selling glass by day and themselves by night.*

Raphael, so anxious when picking me up, had now dropped into slow gear. He slumped in his chair and stretch his legs out. I looked at him. He looked at the lagoon.

We talked for two hours then he walked me back to my apartment a half an hour walk from San Marco. My sister was sleeping in my bedroom. I really had no place to take Raphael but I was determined to fuck him that night if only to get back at Mario. As we were walking back toward my apartment I told him my sister was staying with me and he seemed contented to wait.

"When does she leave?" he asked.

"In two days."

So we would have to wait.

Crossing the little bridge before the Fondemente della Misericordia we stopped and kissed. We didn't stop kissing. My hands were working all over his lean body. His hands were quickly up my dress and underneath my panties. He pulled me back into one of the dead-in alley ways off the street. In the dark alley I felt lost as he pushed me against the ancient stones. He knelt down and started kissing me between my legs. That was it. We had to find some place.

"Where do you live?" I asked him. "Can we go back to your apartment?"

"No, that's impossible. I live with my parents."

Oh yea, all men in Italy live with their parents. Even Casanova apparently.

We snuck into my apartment. I peeked through the door of my bedroom. My sister was asleep. I pulled the door shut. I didn't turn on the lights because I didn't want to wake her up. I didn't want her to wander out in the middle of all this -- hopefully great orgy.

We started on the couch in complete darkness but ended on the floor of my living room, still in complete darkness, fucking on the marble floor. In front of the fireplace. In front of the Frescos. In front of the little angels. Thank God it was dark so they couldn't see what was going on.

# CHAPTER SIX

RAPHAEL filled my heart with love that first night. So I got off on the wrong foot with Mario. Now I found my true love, Rafael. I'm sure he felt the same way about me. I couldn't wait to see him again ... but in the middle of this passionate love affair I had planned a trip with my sister to go to Urbino three hours north of Venice so I couldn't see Raphael for a week. While I was in Urbino I felt so giddy, so much in love. Raphael called me from Venice.

"I feel so ecstatic, so alive," he said joyously into the phone. Those were his words. Ecstatic. How could I not fall in love with someone who was as happy about life as I was?

After coming home to Venice, I put my sister on a plane and ran, literally ran to meet Raphael in the square. The plan was to meet him under the bell tower. I wore a white dress cut low to show off my seducing equipment.

"You look like an angel," he said to me.

He took my hand and showed me his Venice. We walked along the *Riva degli Schiavoni* to a bar. We sat in the moonlight and talked with my head on his shoulder. What we ate I don't have the faintest idea.

It was June so two or three days a week after Raphael finished working, we went to the beach together. His family had a cabana, like most of the families in Venice have, on Lido Beach the narrow long island that separates Venice and the lagoon from the Adriatic Sea. For three months his family rented a little cabana about six feet by twelve feet with a little porch in front. Every day in the summer the family went at 9:00 in the morning, like a job, to the cabana. At the *Spiaggia Buciatoro* there were hundreds of cabanas in neat rows with about fifty cabanas in each row. Usually the families came in the morning with a packed lunch and spent the day eating, sleeping in lounge chairs, reading, playing cards, swimming in the sea and, of course, getting a tan. A summer tan is very important in Italy and the darker the better. No sunscreen lotion here. The kids played with their toys in the sand or they ran around the playground with swings or kicked a ball on the soccer field. There were restrooms and showers and a bar where you could go for a coffee, a glass of wine, a Panini or a gelato. At the bar there were lounge chairs set out under umbrellas and for the price of a drink you could sit in the chair all afternoon. This was my daily life as I waited for Raphael to get off work.

Raphael's parents came in the morning but would leave around noon to return to their Venice apartment. Meeting Raphael's parents was never an option. I was not that kind of girlfriend. Yet.

Around five thirty Raphael would arrive. We would sit in the lounge chairs by the bar and look out over the Mediterranean. I ordered a second sprint (a combination of Aperol, white wine and soda water) and Raphael ordered an iced tea. We caught the last two hours of sun before we showered and went to one of the restaurants on Lido for dinner. Most nights we ended up at *Il Passatore*, a family restaurant where we ate in the enclosed porch in the back. We'd split a salad, pizza and french fries with mayonnaise, Raphael's favorite and only indulgence. About nine we would go back to my apartment and make love. *I could get used to this life.*

One evening I was on my way to meet Raphael at the Rialto Bridge. As I passed by the vaporetto stop, I saw Mario. He was obviously waiting for someone. He called out to me but I ignored him. He followed me.

"Ciao, how are you?" he said trying to catch my arm. He didn't say my name. He probably didn't even remember my name.

"I'm busy," I said pulling my arm out of his grasp.

"I want to see you again."

From the top of the stairs on the *Rialto Bridge* I could see Raphael in *San Bartholomew* Square. He was waiting for me. Mario turned and saw him too.

"Sorry, I'm with Raphael now," I said before I turned around and walked away. Fuck you I thought.

When we weren't at the beach, Raphael took me all over Venice. We went to a wonderful *Baccari*, a wine and appetizer bar, *Hosteria Letizia*, between the Rialto Bridge and San Polo that served *cicchetti* (appetizers) and the best *ombra*, a red wine for only two Euro a glass. Before dinner we would snack on fried crab claws, *polpette* (meatballs), half boiled eggs with anchovies, fried vegetables and fried octopus, a special Venetian dish.

We ate pizza at *La Birraria* in the square at San Polo, out in the open air under the trees. We sat at night at a café between Rialto Bridge and the food market and watched the boats and the people who strolled back and forth. He took me to the bar at *Europa and Regina* hotel on the Grand Canal. We ordered drinks and sat talking about life and looking at life passing in front of us on the Grand Canal.

On our trips back from Lido we took the Number 82 Vaporetto back to San Marco Square. We stood near the railing and kissed under the moonlight as we passed the lights of Venice. My dream had come true. I was living in Venice. I was in love with a wonderful man.

July 13 is the holiday of Redentore and is celebrated by the city with fireworks. Redentore is a centuries old feast dating back to the mid 1500's when Venice was hit by a horrible plague. It lasted three years and killed over 50,000 people, about a third of Venice's population. When the plague was finally over, the city fathers decided to build a church. The church of *Salute* (Health) was built across from San Marco Square. Now hundreds of boats filled the lagoon with party-goers who ate the traditional Venetian foods. At 11:30 at night fireworks exploded over the lagoon. Raphael and I squeezed in with the thousands of tourists and residents who jam the square to see the fireworks. Life could never be better than it was at that moment.

My birthday is in early August. It was Saturday and Raphael took me to dinner at *Hosteria Letizia.* We had a beautiful meal composed of *castroure,* the purple artichoke heart grown on the islands of the lagoon, spaghetti with cuttlefish ink and tiramisu for dessert and a beautiful bottle of red wine. He took me back to my apartment. We made love. He left to go home as he always did. It was official. We were in love. I was his girlfriend. That was my birthday gift.

By Tuesday Raphael had not called me. He was calling almost every day for the past two months and now nothing. By Friday I was frantic. What was going on with him? I texted a message to him on Saturday at 11:43 in the morning.

"Hi, what's up?"

At 12:04 I got a message back.

"I will be busy all the next month," he wrote back to me.

That was it, that was all his message said. I took off my diamond bracelet and flung it on the floor of my bedroom.

"Fuck. Fuck. Fuck," I yelled before flinging myself on the bed. "Fuck love. I hate fucking love."

An hour later I was on the beach in Lido. This was war and I was taking no prisoners. I laid on my towel, topless with a Brazilian bikini and decided to pick up someone. Anyone. I wasn't going to be treated like that.

There are times when I am convinced that the universe is a benevolent place. That God wants us to be happy. And if we just look and go out into the universe, just what we are looking for will show up. After only two hours of laying on the beach I realized there was, sure enough, a God. And God was benevolent. He gives us just what we are looking for. There he was ... a young man... with golden hair, a sumptuous body and a sweet smile.

# CHAPTER SEVEN

LYING on my back I looked at the ocean and saw a young man walk by me. He was gorgeous. Tall, about six feet one, with short blondish hair and a body. What can I say about his body? Perfect is a good word. Sexy is also another good word. Like you want to run your tongue all over it and taste every single cell that made up this perfect man. He saw me looking at him and came up behind me. He sat on the sand about three feet away from me. The beach was crowded with people lying about a foot away from each other. I turned my head to look at him. I looked at his feet. I was afraid to look anywhere else. Just his feet were enough. I slid my arm down so I could peek over my shoulder to get a look at his face. He was looking at me, smiling. I stared right back actually hoping that my sunglasses were hiding my eyes. We continued our eye exchange for about ten minutes. He wasn't making his move. Nothing ventured, nothing gained.

I got up (topless) and swayed my ass into the ocean but not before I turned around and gave him THE LOOK. He took the bait and followed me. I went out until the wave less water hit my shoulders. I turned around and smiled suggestively at this young Apollo in front of me. I was bold that day. Raphael's rejection made me bold.

"Ciao," I said. "What's your name?"

"Andrea," he answered.

We spoke in Italian for a few minutes in the ocean. Then we went back to my towel and started kissing. Yes, as easy as that. In front of a crowd of about five hundred people we were going for it. The only thing that prevented us from having sex right there was my Brazilian bikini and five hundred spectators. I suspect that even on a Lido beach in Italy you would get arrested for having sex (I was wrong about this but that's in a later chapter). I gave him my address and we made plans to meet at my apartment at seven o'clock that night.

Serves Raphael right. The little fucker. Now I'm going to fuck someone else. Someone really hot. And more importantly, younger.

That night at a quarter to seven I leaned out my bedroom window to look if I could see Andrea walking down the Fondementa della Misericordia. The street name mean Street of Mercy. And mercy me, I hoped I was going to get some good stuff tonight. From my window

I could see all the way down the canal that ran next to the street and out to the north lagoon. I watched every person crossing the bridge impatiently waiting for Mr. Apollo to walk over the bridge. Finally, at seven o'clock on the dot, Andrea, with his light almost Fred Astaire-like walk came over the bridge. I waited for him to push my door bell downstairs (hopefully he would be pushing my real bell upstairs pretty soon). I buzzed open the door and went to my foyer and waited for him to come up the stairs. I saw his head first. His head was bent down looking at his feet. He looked up, saw my face and smiled. I will always remember that smile until the day I die. It was everything a smile should be -- hopeful and confident and ecstatically happy like he just hit the lottery. He walked up to me with so much confidence and kissed me. We kissed, standing there at the top of the stairs for a long time. Finally, I took his hand and led him into my living room.

We sat on the sofa. He kissed me. He kissed me for a long time. At this point I have to mention that Italian men are GREAT kissers. I think this comes from the fact that Italian women are a lot more chaste than American women. Sometimes the only sexual satisfaction an Italian male gets is from kissing. I had an Italian boyfriend once and we kissed, nonstop, for five hours on a bench in Assisi. Yes, that holy hometown of St. Francis of Assisi. The entire kissing session was watched by an old woman from her window. She only chose to yell at us after we finished and were walking away. It's very common to see a couple kissing in the park for hours. Italians they

KNOW how to kiss. Yea, Italian men and kissing. A great combo. I forgot how enjoyable kissing can be. It's not something we spend a lot of time doing in America any more. We like to get down to business and then get on to our real business -- making money. The most important thing to an American man is money -- that is how he is judged by society. In Italy the most important thing is sex, that's how an Italian man is judged by himself and his friends. How many conquests he has had. What a great lover he is – that is what is important in Italy.

Andrea and I spent the first thirty minutes kissing and grinding our hips and caressing each other's body on my sofa. Andrea was a great kisser. In fact, I would say at this point in my life, he was the best kisser I ever knew. He had a way of gently devouring my lips. A great combination of tenderness and hunger.

My dress came off.

His pants came off.

Venice is great, I thought. I'm really going to like living here. The other thought that entered my mind was try, try and try again. The third one was a hit. A homerun. Mario didn't work, ok. Raphael didn't work, ok. Now I had Andrea. And this was going to work.

After a twenty minute rest we went into my bedroom.

We made love again. With Andrea it was more like making love, with Raphael and Mario it was hot steamy sex. But with Andrea I floated on my bed. Despite my asking Andrea to stay the night at eleven-thirty he went home. What is it with Italian men, are they on a curfew like Cinderella? I tenderly kissed him goodbye at my front door then ran to my bedroom window. I blew him kisses from my window before he quickly walked down the street and disappeared into the night.

Raphael? Who's Raphael? And I don't even know anyone named Mario.

The best way to forget one man is to start having sex with another one. And preferably even hotter and younger than the one you're trying to forget.

# CHAPTER EIGHT

MONEY -- it's an important issue in life. Let's talk about money. Our lives usually revolve around the getting of money and then the spending of money. Or maybe it's the other way around. We spend money, then we worry about ways to make more money to pay the new bills.

In Venice the rent for my apartment was a thousand Euro a month. I came over with twenty thousand dollars which when converted into Euros was around fifteen thousand Euros. That is a little over a thousand Euro a month. With my expensive apartment I would be lucky to get by for one year. So I started to think of ways to make money. But I was an illegal alien. Legally I had no right to work in Italy. And finding a job is tough in Italy even if you're Italian.

My first idea was to be a street entertainer. I would dress up like an 18th century courtesan with my boobs hanging out of my top. That was sure to make me money. I bought a sewing machine and made an appropriate dress with my boobs mostly out of the dress. I bought a blond wig and -- viola -- I was on the streets. I positioned myself on one of the bridges on the Riva degli Schavoni. People came and took pictures but no one gave me money. I was there for about an hour before the police came and said I needed a permit. So my streetwalking days were over.

My next idea was to teach English. I put up flyers on several bulletin boards around the city. This is a common practice in Venice. There are several places where people tack up flyers for work, apartments and English lessons. My first pupil was a 13 year old Polish boy who had just moved to Italy with his mother who married an Italian man. He needed to study English because he didn't know any English and all of his classmates had been studying English since they were seven years old. English is now taught from the first year of school until graduation in Italy.

He came three times a week right after school. He was a cute and rather plump boy. He dragged himself up the stairs to my apartment and plopped himself down at my dining room table.

"How are you?" I asked in English.

"*Stanco*", he mumbled looking down at the table, "exhausted".

I gave him juice and cookies and taught him some English.

I slowly picked up some other pupils. A man who worked in a restaurant needed to improve his English for his job. An older man who just wanted to learn English to give him something to do. He was retired and remembered as a young boy the American soldiers who came to Venice after World War II saying "Come on". Another pupil was a young man from Treviso who wanted to practice his English and every week he would read from an English book while I listened and corrected his pronunciation. Maybe I would make a hundred Euro a week, but often I would only make twenty-five Euro because people would miss a class or stop all together. The way things were going I wasn't going to make the twelve hundred Euro a month I needed to live and eat by teaching. Venice was great but how was I ever going to afford to stay here? I had the boyfriend, I had the apartment but most of my time I tried to think up ways to make money. I wanted more than anything to stay in Venice forever.

# CHAPTER NINE

**ANDREA** was so hot I thought he might only be a one night stand. And after the disasters I had with Mario and Raphael I was thinking all Venetian men just want a quick fuck and then they move on. But my routine with Andrea quickly became established. Andrea's family had a small store and he worked there six days a week. So Andrea's only time with me was Saturday night at seven o'clock until midnight. It was the five hours I savored each week. But it was only five hours every week. And I had a lot of free time on my hands. Even I, a certifiable beach baby, can only spend so much time at the beach. Despite my infatuation with Andrea, in the back of my mind I was expecting him to drop me so I was open to other relationships. I didn't want to be left unexpectedly jolted like I was with Raphael.

Then after a month Raphael called. I took his call but quickly told him I had another lover.

"It didn't take you very long," he replied shocked that I did not wait around for him.

I didn't mention to him that it only took three hours from the time I got his last text message until I met Andrea on the beach. Faster than you think, I thought to myself. His little girlfriend, whoever the bitch was, was now gone, but he wasn't getting me back. I wasn't going to be his 'when nobody else is around I'll go out with you girl'.

He asked me to go to the mountains with him. Sorry, no can do. He was persistent.

Raphael. A pretty name isn't it. So now I'll tell you about Raphael. Things I didn't know when I first met him but now I knew what I was dealing with. Raphael is a Casanova. The first and legendary Casanova was born in Venice. Today Italy is overloaded with Casanovas. In Venice, where Casanova perfected his craft about four hundred years ago, there is an explosion of irresistible lovers. He is an inspiration to men. Probably all men want to be a Casanova somewhere in their heart. I've met many Casanovas who weren't Italian. Let's face it – Casanova is fun. Who wouldn't like to make love to hundreds of women? Casanova, himself said, that he was in love with every woman he made love to. That's the point. It wasn't just sex with him or numbers. It was beautiful moments of love, when love consumes every part of your being -- physical, mental, spiritual -- that was what Casanova wanted. He pursued it again and again trying to find his true love. The problem was he found a lot of true loves. I think Raphael, like Casanova, was a man who was always on the hunt for true love. He just never finds anyone quite up to all his expectations. Or maybe he finds too many of them. Or perhaps he is scared that if he finds his true love she won't be true to him. Or maybe he just gets bored easily.

Before I go on with Raphael, I should say something about Italian men in general. Well, my take anyway. You have to remember that Italy is a country where 99% of the population is Catholic. They are taught, from the very beginning of their lives, that there are basically only two types of women -- the VIRGIN Mary and Mary Magdalene. All women are therefore in either one category or another. And no woman is a combination of the two. It's against the law of physics like expecting to find the sun and the moon to be the same thing. You marry the Virgin Mary and you fuck Mary Magdalene. The amazing thing about the Virgin Mary is that, as everyone knows, she is the mother of Jesus, but she is still a virgin. Unbelievable, but accepted. Every Italian man, of course, thinks of his mother is a virgin. The other interesting fact about Jesus' story is how little his earthly father, Joseph, played in his life. He is a man in the background, who dies early leaving his wife to follow Jesus around as he troops through Israel. She is the unselfish mother who does whatever she can to make sure her son is taken care of – which is the protocol for all Italian mothers. While

Jesus was preaching, the Virgin Mary, no doubt, was back at the camp ironing his robe with a stone. This is an important fact because like Joseph most fathers in Italy are simply the background music in the family. It is mama who is the center of life. The most spoken word in the Italian language is "mama". Whether you're two years old or sixty -- mama is the big Kahuna in Italy.

Raphael was honest. This is what I liked best about him. He told me from the beginning that the only woman he ever loved was his mother. The other thing he told me is that he hated all women. This he mentioned to me one day at the beach when he was preparing me for the drop. I didn't realize he was going to drop me then and didn't think too much of what he was saying. The thing about Raphael was that there was a part of him that liked to dominate over women, to control them. But he, like most Italian men, are really sweethearts. Their mothers, for all their controlling, do make their sons into sweet, kind, caring and very clean and helpful people. They can cook, clean and iron clothes (sheets & T-shirts & socks are still ironed in Italy – when was the last time you saw your iron). This is what is wonderful about Italian men but also the problem. A heartbreaking sweetie. That's pretty hard to be but I have to say Raphael had the system down to an art.

When Raphael was seventeen years old he had fallen for a girl. He was in love for the first time. The relationship (one kiss) lasted four weeks. Then the girl dropped him for his friend. At that point Raphael resolved never to have his heart crushed again. From then on it was just a game. He could act the part of a dedicated enthusiastic lover but he never allowed himself to go over the line. He never really loved anyone. He never allowed himself to love anyone.

In the movie, *Dangerous Beauty*, a movie about a courtesan in Venice in the late 1500's, the mother tells her daughter who is training to become a courtesan, "Love love, but do not love the man or you will be in his power."

These words meant for a young girl about to become a courtesan but they were words that Raphael lived by. He loved love but he was never in any woman's power. He loved the thought of being in love.

It wasn't until the age of nineteen that Raphael lost his virginity. To a hooker in Thailand. Thailand is a mystical place for Italian men. "A large brothel on the beach", Raphael once explained to me. Sex for five bucks. But this was too easy for a true Italian lover. He liked the chase. The pursuit. He was an expert hunter after all.

Raphael liked the romance surrounding the act of sex itself. He loved making women fall in love with him. Like most Italian men Raphael spent his twenties mostly not having sex. He was still in training. Italian girls want marriage and are not willing to give away the goods without the understanding that marriage will follow. There are the families to consider. An unending barrage of eyes watching you – parents, aunts, uncles, grandparents, neighbors and all with advice about what to do with your life. Almost everyone in town knows you. Nothing can be done in secrecy. Your bed might as well be in the middle of San Marco Square because everybody will know what you are doing.

It wasn't until he got his job at the glass factory that he got the chance or the chances he wanted. The first thing he had to do was to learn English. The foreign girls are there, ready for picking up, but they won't respond to someone who speaks no English. They need talking to. A lot of talking to. Sometimes the girls need days and days and sweet phrases and magical nights under the Venice moon. Others need only a few drinks.

Raphael had his preferred prey. These women he found to be the easiest and perhaps the most interesting. A woman of around forty was his preferred prey. She was usually divorced with two children. She was attractive, had a good job and took care of herself. She wanted magic on her two weeks away from her job in Milwaukee or New Jersey and Raphael gave her that. Depending on her projected value to him he either took her to the chairs in front of San Marco Square (the lowest value which is where I was taken) or for a drink at the Austrian bar standing up (he wasn't really sure about her so wanted to spend as little money as possible) or to the bar across from the Ducale Palace where his brother worked and where he got a heavily discounted price (if he paid at all). A really important date got taken to the bar at the Europa and Regina hotel where one could sit on the Grand Canal and look at the church of Salute.

After a few days or weeks of sex she was off back to her own country. The next night Raphael was again down at the square scouting new prey.

The great thing about Raphael was he sent emails to all of his girlfriends. They would become useful later when he took his winter trip (he was off from his job for three months in the winter). He went to Florida, California, New York, England, Russia, Japan, and Australia and anywhere else he might have an old girlfriend-in-waiting. Many of them dreamed of marriage. They wanted to escape from their life and live in this dream world called Venice. He, of course, put them off but still he showed me their letters to him saying how they dreamed of being tied up to a bed. They sent pictures of their tits and asses. He gladly showed his friends the pictures. They were like baseball cards. Things to be collected and shown off to his friends. Women, for these men, were not humans but merely things to be acquired and bragged about to their friends. The woman herself was not important, only her face value (what she looked like and what she did in bed).

Sex for many men was more about the competition with their friends. Men all around the world have only two things to talk about -- sports and sex. In Venice two men rarely meet without the topic of who they were doing or trying to do came up.

So Raphael's "other" girlfriend from Australia or America or wherever she had come from was gone and Raphael needed to get laid again. Naturally, I came to his mind. My attractiveness was that I was in town. Raphael taught me many lessons. This was the first. A normal girl, which I was before I met Raphael, thinks a certain way -- one man, one love, that's it. She is faithful to him. He is faithful to her. But Raphael was teaching me another way of living. This is Raphael's first lesson -- I will fuck other girls but it doesn't affect our relationship at all. I will still always come back to you.

After a few weeks of Raphael's persistent calling I went to Cortina with him. I think he assumed that I ended my relationship with this other guy, but as you know, I didn't. I began to live my life like Raphael lived his life. I would take my pleasure with him but I would cut myself off from any real emotion for him.

I had true affection for Andrea but I only saw Andrea on Saturdays and Andrea was not interested in expanding our relationship to anything else. Andrea was a mama's boy and always would be. Raphael would take me out to dinner two or three nights a week. So I was learning how to play the game of love in Venice.

# CHAPTER TEN

SEPTEMBER was hot and my relationships with Andrea and Raphael both went on but I was stifled with both men. I was quickly falling in love with Andrea but he stuck to his once a week routine. And he was younger than me. Don't fall in love with him I told myself every week. He's too young for you. He's too innocent for you.

We would lie in bed after making love and sing songs. You know really stupid songs like "She'll be coming around the mountain when she comes" which for some reason Andrea knew. The American culture permeates everywhere. Andrea knew and loved American movies like 'Casablanca' and 'Singing in the Rain'. In fact, Gene Kelly was one of his favorite actors. He knew old movies like the 'Best Years of Our Lives'. Every week he would come over, we'd fuck first, eat dinner, watch a movie and fuck again. Then he'd go home. Our routine never varied.

We composed a list of our favorite movies. His all-time favorite was '*Gallipoli*'. Mine, as anyone who has known me from the age of eight will tell you is '*Gone with the Wind.*' I'm just crazy for Scarlett and in fact wrote a sequel called "*Scarlett's Other Life*" where Scarlett gets married three more times (and yes Ashley ends up as one of her husbands but she isn't happy being married to him). Scarlett learned, like me, the fantasy and the reality of man are completely different.

So my life with Andrea proceeded at a slow but steady pace. One Sunday he took me and his best friend to Feltre, a small town in the Dolomite Mountains. We walked around the town, ate pizza, ate gelato and tried to remember the names of the seven dwarfs. How I adored my Andrea. But Andrea never asked me out on a Sunday again. I think he was falling in love with me too but when his friend met me I was diagnosed as too old. Of course Andrea kept on fucking me but as to anything else ...

Raphael was steadily in the picture. While Andrea had practically no experience with women, Raphael had tons. And he was playing his part of not getting me to fall in love with him. He was mostly cold. Persistent, but cold. He had too many girls fall in love with him and try to pressure him into marriage and he did not want that to happen again.

So I was basically frustrated. One day I was walking home from the beach through the north side of the island through the Castello neighborhood because being late summer the Riva degli Schavoni on the southern side of Venice is like walking in hell. No two ways about it, it is hell on that street on summer afternoons in Venice. So I preferred taking the dark alleys back to my apartment by way of the Arsenale and the hospital. I was just crossing the bridge to Fondementa Nuove near the hospital when I turned around and saw a man watching me as I walked up the steps. He was smiling. I had noticed him a few minutes before in the Campo of Saints Giovanni and Paolo and thought he was cute.

I was wearing a very short skirt with my bathing suit (a thong) underneath, so I can imagine his view as I walked up the stairs of the bridge. I waited for him and we walked together for a while without talking. Finally he asked me where I was going.

"Fondemente della Misericordia," I told him. "And where are you going?" I asked in Italian.

"I'm going there too," he said.

We walked together again in silence until we got to my street. Then he followed me about ten paces behind. When I got to my door I opened it and left it ajar for him. He followed me at a distance up the stairs. I left the door open to my apartment and went to the bathroom and stripped and got into the shower. He came in my apartment, stood at the bathroom door and watched me as I took a shower.

With him still standing in the bathroom doorway I got out and dried myself off. We still didn't say a word. He moved away from the door as I walked out of the bathroom to my bedroom. I kneeled on my bed.

"Do you have any toys?" he asked me in Italian.

I thought this was a strange question. Yes, I had toys but I had never used them when I was with a man before.

"I know you have some," he said and then he opened the table by my bed. Yes, he found a dildo and gave it to me.

"Use it," he said.

I took the dildo and started playing with myself.

"Don't you want to touch me?" I asked him.

He shook his head no.

"Come fuck me," I said.

"I can't," he said, "I'm married."

Just like an Italian. The man's married. He'll come to a strange girl's apartment to watch a naked girl masturbate but won't touch her.

He undid his pants and played with his cock. I laid down on the bed to offer to suck him off but he wouldn't let me touch him. He jerked off on my face.

Well, technically he was faithful, but I doubt if his wife had witnessed the scene she would have thought so.

He never even kissed me.

For the next month, on Mondays, I walked by the Fondementa Nuove vaporetto and there he was hanging out in front of the bar. He would follow me home and we continued our strange, non-touching affair for a month. But one Monday I just decided not to go by the Fondementa Nuove. I never saw him again. I don't even think he told me his name or if he did, it was probably a fake name.

# CHAPTER ELEVEN

ANDREA was reliable. Every Saturday night at seven o'clock on the dot he was at my apartment. And just as promptly he was gone by midnight. A male Cinderella I suppose, he might turn into a pumpkin if he wasn't home by twelve-thirty.

Raphael, on the other hand, was reliably unreliable. I'd see him three nights in a row and then not for another week. So I had a lot of free time. One Tuesday I went to the beach and around three o'clock took the vaporetto back from Lido to Fondementa Nuove. It's a long ride on the vaporetto from Lido to Fondemente Nuove, about forty-five minutes. The vaporetto travels along the backside of Venice and is not nearly as beautiful or interesting as the vaporetto that goes by the Giardini and San Marco

Square, so it's a boat with lots of locals. The boat takes the long trip around Santa Elena, a new enclave of Venice built in the 19th century. The 42 vaporetto goes past the backside of the Arsenale, past the island of San Michele, the cemetery island where all the dead are buried. The boat was packed as it usually is from Lido in the middle of the day. Everyone was coming home from their day at the cabana. I had a seat but gave it up to an older lady. I went to the deck of the boat which was full with people when I noticed a very good-looking man next to the rail. He had a long pony-tail and was very tanned. I looked at him. He looked back at me. We were both wearing sunglasses so it's not so obvious we were staring at each other but we were. Neither one of us was going to be the first to look away. When the vaporetto stopped at San Pietro more people pushed onto the deck. There was a crush of people on the boat. The man moved next to me. I pressed up against him as though it was the crowd pressing me into him. He moved his hand down my thigh. He rubbed my thigh with his finger. We were no longer staring at each other because we were standing side my side. A few minutes later his finger was under my skirt and rubbing my swimming suit bottoms. I did nothing but let him continue to feel me up on the vaporetto with people all around us.

When the vaporetto stopped at Fondemente Nuove I got off. He got off.

"Where are you going?" he asked me.

This was a very familiar line. Is this what all Venetian men asked women they were trying to pick up? I told him I lived on Fondementa della Misericordia.

"Me too," he said.

We walked together. His name was Raphael. I almost laughed out loud. He was forty-one and had long curly brown hair to his shoulders. A nice face. Big lips. Big kissable lips.

"Do you want to come up to my apartment for a minute," I asked him.

"Yes, but my girlfriend lives on this street. I'll follow you. Leave the door open," he told me.

A few minutes later we were in my bed naked. He had a rubber, which all men carry around with them these days (all but Mario who preferred to take risks).

We fucked. A half an hour later he was gone.

"This is a one-time thing," he tells me at the door before he left. "I have a girlfriend."

OK, how many times does he have to tell me that? I would often see him in the streets of Cannaregio. There was always a ciao and a smile and but nothing else with Raphael number two. Like he said, it was a one time and one time only deal.

# CHAPTER TWELVE

**IN** between my little sexual adventures I was actually falling in love with Andrea. He was always so polite, so pleasant. And in bed he was so pleasing. Andrea's first and only sexual experience before me had been only a few years earlier when he was twenty-five. Andrea may not have had a lot of physical experience but he did watch a lot of porno and he was willing to try anything. Andrea was learning fast. As time went by our lovemaking was more passionate and nastier. We reveled in our sweetness and our nastiness.

For the five hours a week I spent with him I was content. More than content, I was head over heels in love. When he left I couldn't sleep knowing I'd have to wait another week before I could see him again, before I could touch him again. Patience. Waiting. That's a hard thing to learn. I was teaching English a little but not enough to occupy too much of my time. Summer was over. It was turning cold. I was bored.

I started getting text messages from an unknown source.

"Hi, I saw you in the square and think you are so beautiful."

"I want to meet you."

"You are driving me crazy. I have to see you."

All these text messages were signed Stefano.

Stefano, I didn't know a Stefano. In total, I received about twenty texts from this mystery man before I replied.

"Who are you?" I wrote. "How did you get my telephone number?"

"A friend of mine knows you. He gave it to me."

"Who is this friend of yours?" I asked.

"I can't tell you. I promised I wouldn't tell you," he answered.

I was convinced it was Raphael. Who else could it be? Now the bastard was giving my number out to his friends.

"Let's meet," he texted.

"OK, but tell me who gave you my number. I won't go out with you until you tell me the name of your friend."

"Meet me tonight at ten o'clock and I'll tell you."

I agreed to meet him.

That bastard Raphael. I am going out with his friend. And I'm going to fuck his friend. But first I had to write a text to Raphael to let him know how I felt.

"You bastard. Why did you give my number out to your friend?"

Raphael called me up and denied knowing anything. I didn't believe him.

At ten o'clock I went to the *Campo of Santa Maria Formosa* and waited in front of the church.

A man walked up. He was not my type, a little too much pasta, but I had revenge on my mind so he became my type.

"So, who is this friend of yours?" I asked.

"I can't tell you," he answered.

"Well, I guess I can't fuck you then."

"You mean you will only have sex with me if I tell you my friend's name."

"Yep, that's what I mean."

He pushed his lips together while he thought about it for ten seconds.

The cock is stronger than friendship.

"OK, it's Mario."

Fuck. It was Mario. Asshole Mario. And I just called Raphael a bastard because I thought it was him.

Well, a deal is a deal, so I followed Stefano, who told me his name was really Dario, back to the restaurant which he was managing not far from San Zaccaria. It was late and there were only a few tables of people remaining in the restaurant. He sat me down and offered me dinner.

I ordered spaghetti with clams. A pretty little waitress about twenty years old from Slovania brought me the plate. She smiled at me as she set the plate down. She remained standing next to the table and looked at me with livid curiosity. I ate alone. Stefano/Dario (whatever his name was) went into the kitchen with the waitress. What were they doing? What am I doing here with some guy I don't even want to fuck, eating dinner alone while he's in the kitchen with some chic?

By the time I finished my meal the restaurant was empty. Stefano/Dario let the waitress and two cooks out and locked the door behind them. We were alone in the restaurant. He turned off a few lights and led me back to a table. I sat on the table with my ass near the edge. He kissed me for a few moments before I leaned back with my head near the salt and pepper shakers. He fucked me on the table while he was standing. He was good but I was so mad at Mario and couldn't wait to leave.

We finished. We kissed. I put on my clothes to leave. I was impatiently waiting for him to open the door. I wanted out of there.

"Wait," he tells me, "I'll walk you home."

"No thanks, I prefer to walk by myself".

"Come on, let me take you home."

Trying to change the subject I asked, "So where's Mario?"

"He's taking two young Russian girls to Rimini this weekend."

I was hoping to get out with just a quick fuck. But now I was fuming mad at Mario again. Two Russian girls. How jealous I am of Russian girls. They make me crazy jealous.

Stefano/Dario came home with me that night and spent the night. In the morning I told him he had to leave.

"What, just like that," he said holding his clothes I had just thrown at him.

"Yes, you have to go now. I'm busy this morning."

"Can I see you again?"

"I don't know. Just go now."

Finally I got him out of my apartment, closing the door on his face.

I called Raphael to apologize. He laughed that I had made the mistake. He said he would never give my number to one of his friends. This I learned was true. Raphael was very protective of his conquests. If his girls fucked other guys his myth he created about himself to his friends that he was a great Casanova would have exploded. They were just sluts who would sleep with anyone. Raphael prized himself on seducing the uncatchable woman. The elusive woman. The harder the woman was to catch, the more attracted he was to her. He was Casanova's understudy after all. And me, I didn't know what I was or was about to become.

# CHAPTER THIRTEEN

**OK,** I'm a slut (**S**ingle **L**ady **U**nder **T**ransformation). I think that point has been established by this time. But sluts can fall in love too. Andrea. My passion for Andrea grew with each week we stayed together. Every Saturday Andrea showed up at my apartment like a standing invitation. Summer became fall and fall became winter and Andrea still came. There were a few problems with Andrea. First of all, he was younger than me. He lived with his family and except for me appeared to have the most boring of lives. He never went out. He worked from seven in the morning until one in the afternoon. He went home ate lunch with his family (mama) and watched TV. Three days a week he went to the gym to work out for two hours in the afternoon which is what gave him his spectacular body. He'd eat dinner with his family at seven and watch his American TV programs -- CSI, Desperate Housewives, etc. By ten he was asleep in his twin bed, the same twin bed he'd been sleeping in since he was 5 years old. He read comic books. Every Sunday, his only day off, he went on some excursion with either his mother or father. I was a little suspicious of this. Why was he always busy on Sundays? Did my sweet Andrea have a Sunday girlfriend? One Sunday I had to go to Padua to give an English lesson. The night before Andrea told me he was going to Padua with his mother to a comic book convention. I didn't think anything about it but when we pulled into Padua station I stayed in my seat to let the rush of people off. My student in Padua picked me up at the train station but he was always late so I was in no hurry to get off the train. I was looking out the window when I looked up. Andrea was walking to the door and behind him was his mother. We quickly looked at each other but we both looked away acting like we didn't recognize each other.

My heart dropped. I got off the train and smoked a cigarette. Three in fact. Andrea didn't want to admit he knew me. Andrea was embarrassed for me to meet his mother. Of course he was, anyone could tell I was older than him. Then I realized Andrea really was a mama's boy. He was the first born. He was mama's good little boy. But really he was a very nasty boy fucking me every week with such relish. My dreams of Andrea got readjusted that day. There would be no happy ever after with him.

He would never allow himself to be in love with me. I just wasn't the proper material.

The next time I saw him neither of us mentioned the train incident. It remains an unspoken topic even to this day.

Andrea's falling was Raphael's rising.

Raphael was amused by my thinking he had given my name out. And the thought that I was fucking other men loosen Raphael up. He no longer had to fey disinterest. We could now have fun.

And fun we had.

Raphael had a particular fixation. An unusual fetish of putting large candles up his ass. I became his courtesan, the woman he could share his secrets with and we played with his candles. This kind of stuff you don't do with everyone. So we became good buddies after this.

The one problem for me was still how to make a living in Venice. I brought this up for the fourteenth time with Raphael.

"You should become a courtesan," he casually says to me as though he telling me I should get chicken today at the market. Matter-of-fact. A natural conclusion.

"A courtesan?" I asked.

"Yes, a courtesan. All women want to be courtesans."

"Really? And what's so great about being a courtesan?"

"Freedom. They are free. If you get married your husband can tell you what to do. He can spend your money. A courtesan, in the old days, was a very educated woman. She specialized in the art of seduction. She dressed beautifully and men adored her. She made a lot of money, she could become rich."

Well so far he didn't say anything that didn't sound great.

"A courtesan is just a fancy name for a whore," I said.

"No, there you are wrong. A whore is cheap. She'll sleep with anyone. A courtesan chooses her lovers. They supply her with money and she supplies them with love," he answered me.

"You mean sex."

"There is sex, yes, but there's so much more than sex."

"Well, all that is very nice but that's five hundred years ago. There aren't courtesans anymore."

"Yes there are. And you could be one."

I looked at him dumfounded. Was he serious? Could he really be suggesting this to me like a career choice. So funny, when I was going to college I didn't see a major in Courtesan or would it be Courtesaning like Accounting or Marketing. An American girl in the twenty-first century becoming a courtesan. I don't think so.

# CHAPTER FOURTEEN

**ONE** afternoon I was walking home from Santa Elena. As I was walking down my street I noticed a teenage boy behind me. I really didn't think anything about him, he was too young. A kid. As I stopped to open my door he stood behind me. He smiled. I smiled. He must be going to visit someone in my building I thought. Perhaps my neighbor's son. I opened the door and he followed me. If he had been older I would have been suspicious about him following me. But he was around sixteen way too young to be interested in me. I walked up the stairs to the first floor. He was right on my tail. I turned the corner to walk up the second flight of stairs. He was still behind me. He smiled at me again as I looked back at him. He must be going to the apartment on the top floor

I thought. I stopped on my floor to open the outer door of my apartment. He was standing behind me. I opened the inner door to my apartment and turned around to look at him.

"*Que cosa voui?*" I asked. "What do you want?"

"Do you want a massage?" he asked me in Italian.

"*Cosa?*" I asked not sure I heard what he said.

"*Volgio un massagio?*" he repeated.

"Cosa," I answered hesitantly. I wasn't quite getting what he really wanted.

"Do you want a massage?" he repeated.

Oh, ok, now I understand.

"No, thank you," I said before I quickly closed the door.

Young, crazy Italian boys. There will be no massages tonight. Not in this apartment anyway.

That night Raphael came over. As we were sitting on the sofa ready for a night of fun when my buzzer rang. I thought it might be the young boy again. I went to my bedroom window to see who it was.

It was Mario.

Shit, I can't believe it's him.

I went back into the living room.

Raphael asked, "Who is it?"

"It's Mario."

Raphael knew Mario and hated him. All the guys know each other and the competition between who's the real Casanova in town was intense. Mario was younger than Raphael. Mario was an up and comer. And Raphael didn't like that he was up and coming to my apartment.

"What are you going to do?" Raphael asked.

"Nothing. Let him stay downstairs all night for all I care," I said.

A few afternoons later my buzzer rang again.

Oh my God, is it Mario again?

No, it was the young boy who was offering me a massage. I answered the buzzer.

"What do you want?" I asked him.

"Do you want a massage?" he asked.

Too young I thought. That's too dangerous, even in Italy. That's a can of worms I don't want to be involved with. Besides he looks like he has a little gypsy blood in him. He'd probably drug me and steal my money.

Many Italian men have their first experiences with older women. The women their own age are too protected by their families. It's with an older women with experience who are likely to be an Italian man's first sexual partner. They don't practice with their girlfriends like American boys, they want a woman with experience.

One of my boyfriends told me his first experience was with a friend of his mother's. He was nineteen at the time and she was a woman around thirty years older than him. Another man told me his aunt introduced him to sex. Italians are a little crazy when it comes to sex.

Over the next few months, this young man continued to ring my buzzer and once even came to my door.

"Massage?" he always asked.

Italian men, even if they are still boys, are persistent.

One late night I was home alone when Mario again rang my buzzer. Raphael was out with someone and Andrea was at home with his mother.

I was a little drunk so I let Mario come up.

"What do you want?" I asked him when I let him in my door.

"You," he said.

I was not in a good humor and was ready to give it to him. All the frustration I felt with him came spilling out of me.

"Get out," I said.

"I want you."

He pushed his hard body against mine. His hands wrapped around my body.

"No, I want you out of here. You fucking gave my phone number to your friend," I said.

I hadn't seen him since the Stefano/Dario incident.

"What are you talking about?"

"I'm talking about Dario. You gave Dario my telephone number."

"I don't know a Dario," he said.

"Well, he knows you. He told me you gave him my number."

"You're wrong. I only want to see you. My father has been sick. And I've been busy moving."

"You're really incredible. So how were the Russian girls?"

"I don't know any Russian girls."

"Just leave. Go. Now. I want you out of here."

"No you don't. You let me in," he said pushing his way into my apartment.

"Yes I do. Get out."

We struggled until I finally pushed him out the door and slammed it closed.

Bastard. He wasn't getting me again.

"Go with the Russian girls back to Rimini", I yelled through the closed door at him.

It wasn't so much the Russian girls but his pimping me off on his friend that made me so mad at him. And also he was the first man to spoil my dream of love in Venice.

Perhaps now Mario realized I wanted nothing to do with him.

# CHAPTER FIFTEEN

THE Collection. I call this next chapter the collection because it is about a collection of men I had sex with but whose relationships quickly fizzled out.

Severino was a muscle-budging waiter. He worked on Lido and as I walked back from the beach I would pass by the restaurant where he worked. He would be standing by the door watching, his arms crossed in front of him, smiling. A big smile. An ear to ear smile. It was usually around four o'clock when I headed home and he was resting in between the lunch and dinner shifts.

He always said hi to me, in English, when I passed. One day we talked. He was from Venice but lived in Australia with a girlfriend for three years. He had the perfect Australian accent and I thought of him more as

Australian than Italian. But he was 100% Italian. So I invited him to my apartment that night. I had to wait up until one o'clock in the morning because he left work around midnight. It was about an hour ride from Lido to San Marcula, the closest vaporetto stop to my apartment. He proved to be very versatile in bed. For me there are two types of guys -- nasty and not nasty. Severino was a nasty boy. We fucked a couple of hours and then he left. I enjoyed Severino but he was a serious body-builder. That means 24 eggs a day. His whole life revolve around eating a diet to support his massive muscle growth. Andrea also was a body-builder but he was thin with muscles. Severino was huge. Also Severino had a hard time coming. One night I blew him for an hour and nothing. He lived in Mestre and between working and his commute there wasn't any time to have a real relation with him. And I wasn't too happy about getting up at one o'clock at night for sex.

Another piece of the collection was Paulo who was a cook from Sicily. He was young, about twenty years old and a little chubby which guys who work in restaurants often are. When his contract in Venice was up at the restaurant he went back to Sicily and so much for that dalliance.

There was another Stefano. He was from a seaside town not far from Rome. He had dark brown hair and a mole near his lip and looked a little like a young George Hamilton. He lived in Mestre and worked at some government job. He, like so many of the men in Venice, walked the streets at night looking for pick-ups. He followed me one night while I was walking down Strada Nova toward the Ghetto. Sitting on the benches off *Sacca di San Girolamo* was one of my favorite places in Venice. It was a quiet place I had come to know years before and I often went there when I wanted to be alone. There you could look at the island of Murano and the airport on the mainland. And the mountains in the background. It was a busy sea fare and boats whizzed by or stopped at the boat gas station nearby on the dock.

We stuck up a conversation near Santa Fosca church and by the time we reached the bench by the gas station on the lagoon we were kissing. It was night and dark and secluded. I could have asked him back to my apartment but I hesitated. He asked me to give him a blow job there on the bench. I guess those who ask receive. I didn't but I made plans with him for another night. He seduced me with talk about me coming to his hometown for a vacation for a week, but nothing ever came of that.

Another one was a young artist from Sicily. He had black curly hair down to his collar bone. He was built solid, short, and efficient. He was also twenty years old. We met in San Marco square on the benches outside the Doge's Palace. He gave me a little bird made of paper. We walked down to the Arsenale and kissed on the bench in front of the Arsenal Museum. It was a night with a full moon and it was a cool spring evening. He came to my apartment a few times, then he went to Sicily for a month to visit his family. Later I saw him a few times in the square looking for women. I'm sure he found many just like he had found me by giving them his little paper birds.

Now there was hardly a day that went by when I didn't see at least three of my lovers on the streets of Venice. Venice is surprisingly a small town.

# CHAPTER SIXTEEN

**MY** one year anniversary was coming up. It was December and in March my lease would be up. And the twenty thousand I had brought with me from America was down to five thousand. My teaching jobs were sporadic and even on the best months I made only three hundred Euro, hardly enough for my thousand dollar apartment.

I thought I would find a roommate. At least that would make my monthly expenses about six hundred. I didn't want to leave my beautiful apartment. Raphael had a friend who was looking for a room. We struck a deal -- he would rent the bedroom for five hundred a month. I would sleep in the living room. At least this way I could stay in my beautiful apartment.

We had scheduled a day for him to move in, but he didn't show up even though he had already given me the five hundred Euro. I had already made the bed with clean sheets for him so I slept on the sofa. About one o'clock in the morning he came in. But he was not alone. A woman was with him. He moved several boxes of books into the bedroom. I tried to sleep but he and woman stayed up talking until four in the morning. About seven in the morning I heard him leave. But what about the woman? What happened to her? I opened the bedroom door and there she was sleeping on the little sofa in the room. This was a strange. He never mentioned anything about a girl to me. And the girl obviously didn't sleep in the bed with him. This girl slept until one in the afternoon, got up took a shower and left. She never said anything to me. Was this just a pickup? What was going on here?

This friend of Raphael's, Giovanni, had told me he wasn't going to stay in the apartment that month because his ex-wife was going back to Australia and he would be staying at her apartment to take care of their ten-year-old son. Still he said nothing about the woman who was staying in the apartment. In my bed.

A week went by. Giovanni never came back but every night the girl would come to the apartment about two in the morning. She slept until one in the afternoon. When she got up, she showered and left. But Giovanni still didn't call me or mention anything to me about her. Finally I told Raphael about this strange woman who I wasn't even introduced to. Was this normal? Giovanni did finally call me and said she was a friend of his and she needed a place to stay for a few days (it had already been a week). Ok, I thought. I was scheduled to go back to America for Christmas anyway in a few days. She should be gone by the time I get back. I left for two weeks to America and returned New Year's Day about one in the afternoon. I could see that the woman was still there. I tried to call Giovanni. He had gone on a holiday with his son to the south of Italy. The next day at ten o'clock in the morning the woman came home. She was a young girl, about twenty with long black hair. She was dressed in her short black dress, a party dress from the night before.

"Ciao," she said before she disappeared into the bedroom. What was I running here?

Still, the two or four o'clock in the morning arrivals continued. Sometimes there was a man with her. Because the sofa was next to the door, I always heard them come in. About a week later after nights of not sleeping I called Giovanni. This girl has to go, I told him.

"I can't sleep, she comes home early in the morning and there was a man with her."

Giovanni came and got the girl's things when I was out. She was gone, but so was he. So much for getting a roommate.

As March came around Andrea and Raphael's regular routine continued. If I left Venice, they would miss me because even though there were other girls to have sex with, it could be nothing regular. All the Italian girls wanted a commitment and loyalty. The foreign women were short-term alliances, but there could be months between one woman and another. They both liked the regular, noncommittal sex. And I was doing things with them sexually that they couldn't ask just any girl to do. I talked about going home to America. I loved Italy, it was my soul's home. America seemed like a crushing hand around my neck. It's true I could I survive there. It was easy to physically survive in America -- you get a job, you get an apartment, but to spiritually survive -- it was impossible for me. I would rather live in a grass hut in Africa then return to the United States. I had gone home to America after living four years in Europe before when I had left Monte Carlo and it nearly killed me. Coming back to Italy was my life saver. How could I ever go back there again? I might as well be going to my grave.

Andrea was the first to suggest it. I could move to a less expensive apartment or a room and he would give me some money every month to help pay for it. I was shocked at his suggestion. Innocent Andrea, he lived with his parents and made a decent wage, but could he afford to support me -- even partially. I guess he could afford it. He was the one who made the offer.

I saw Raphael a few days later.

"I'm thinking of getting a cheaper apartment," I told him.

"That would be great," he said.

"But even with that I don't think I can make my rent every month."

"Don't worry. I can give you some money to help you pay for it."

And so as easy as that I had two sponsors. Two men willing to support me. Between the two of them I could pay for a smaller apartment. At least I could stay in Italy. I could write. I could make love. It was a better alternative than going back to America. And traffic jams. I guess I was to become a courtesan in Venice after all.

# CHAPTER SEVENTEEN

**ON** March first I looked for a new apartment. The tricky part was getting one that was both convenient to Andrea and Raphael.

Andrea lived by the University and Piazza Roma. Raphael lived by the Opera. The perfect place would be near San Polo, a place close to both of them but not too close to either one.

Both Raphael and Andrea tried to find me an apartment. It was hard to find anything this time of the year. Most of the apartments were rented to students at the University of Venice. The best time to find a room was the beginning or the end of the summer. As my final two weeks in my beautiful palazzo were about to come to an end, I took a temporary border, a young girl, eighteen, from England. She was in Venice for a month to study the piano. She was staying in a room, but it was to be occupied the last week she was in Venice. She came to spend the last week with me in my apartment. My money was dangerously low. I was down to my last thousand. She gave me $150 for a week. She slept in my bed, I slept on the sofa and mourned the last week in my beautiful palazzo.

The first apartment I looked at would have been perfect. Near San Polo it was close enough to both Andrea and Raphael to make it convenient for both of them. It was also far enough away that there would probably be no inconvenient meetings with one when I was with the other. It was a small single room rented by a man in his early forties. He was a marathon runner, as was Raphael, so I mentioned this. Mentioning I already had a boyfriend probably ruined my chances of getting the apartment. As he was showing me the room another girl from Padua, around twenty who was with her father, came to look at the apartment. I said I wanted the room but the man seemed more interested speaking with the father than with me. Perhaps it was the young girl or the fact they were Italian and I was a foreigner that I didn't get the room. Being American I tend to think we come with a pedigree but I was, after all, just a foreigner, an illegal alien.

I was desperate and no other rooms seemed available in Venice. Mestre was an option but living in Mestre was like living in America, an unattractive alternative. So I looked in Lido. It was nearly summer and I was in Lido every day in the summer anyway so maybe that would be a good choice.

The first room I looked at had two bedrooms and a little garden. One bedroom was shared by a Chinese man and woman. The second bedroom I would have to share with another girl. She was a student at the University from Ancona. But when I called back the next day she never answered my phone call.

I had two days left before I had to move out. The girl who was staying at my apartment told me about a bed in a room shared by three girls near San Lio. It was a misshaped apartment with three boys and three girls sharing two bedrooms and one bathroom. This would have been a nightmare. It was on the top floor of the attic of the palazzo. I couldn't imagine myself living in such a crazy place.

The day before my last day in the palazzo I called about a shared room in Lido. Two young girls from Slovenia met me at the vaporetto in Lido. They took me to the room which was in a modern apartment building behind the Hotel du Bain. There I met my new roommate, a pretty girl of eighteen who came from Marche. My other roommates in the apartment was a young boy, Arturo, from Sardinia and a girl from Trente. All students. All eighteen years old. I guess I was to be the mama of the bunch.

The first day I moved in the young boy told me not to come in the kitchen because he was taking some pictures. But I thought he said come in the kitchen, I want you to take some pictures of me. (So my Italian isn't perfect). I went into the kitchen and there he was naked with a camera. I very calmly took the camera from him and said OK I was ready to take some pictures. His shyness and embarrassment made me realize I had made a mistake in my translation. But I did take some pictures of him and we became friends.

The next day Arturo and I were in the kitchen when he suggested we watch a movie. Halfway through the movie I figured out the movie was about a gay guy and that Arturo was gay. He proceeded to tell me about his great first love with an older man and his various love affairs since then.

My young girl roommates looked at me with a combination of envy and fear. Who was this woman who lived in their apartment? When one of the girls introduced me to a friend of hers she said, "She is an adventurer."

Okay, I'll take that description.

Quickly adjusting to my new home, Andrea and Raphael continued their weekly visits. The only difference was now they had the right to visit me. Both were paying me to keep the apartment. Andrea came on Saturdays nights as usual. He made the hour trip over to Lido and the only difference was he now left at ten instead of midnight to make the hour trip home.

It was April. A cold dampness still hung on to the days and nights. Raphael did not come out to Lido so often. He asked me to come to Venice to meet him. One day he did come out to Lido and he met Arturo.

As I introduced Arturo to Raphael, Arturo stood motionless and speechless. Even after Raphael said hello and went over to him to shake his hand, Arturo remained mute. It was love at first sight for Arturo and the only thing Arturo could do was to retreat into his bedroom without saying a word.

When I saw Arturo the next day the first words out of this mouth were, "*O Dio*, he is so beautiful. I couldn't say anything I was so struck by his beauty."

Arturo was fascinated by Raphael. He wanted to fuck my boyfriend.

# CHAPTER EIGHTEEN

**APRIL,** a cold and rainy month, was replaced by May and a sunnier and warmer Lido appeared. Lido became the town of Wisteria. Many beautiful houses had been built in the late 19<sup>th</sup> and early 20<sup>th</sup> century on the island as summer vacation homes. They were large summer houses for the rich who came to spend the summer on Lido and the gardens were heavily planted with wisteria. Now these hundred year old plants dominated the gardens growing over fences and up to the roofs of the houses. The town was veiled under layers of purple. Bicycles were abundant here and life was slower and easier than in Venice only ten minutes away by boat. The famous resort days from a hundred years ago were mostly over but the feeling of summer woke up the streets that were sleepy and barren during the cold, rainy winter months.

Early morning I walked along the beach to my gym about a mile away from my home. After my workout, I began my morning ritual of sunbathing on the nearby deserted beach in front of the Hotel du Bain.

About three weeks into the month of May, the weather was hot. One Saturday I was at the public beach near the bar and the observation walk. It was early, around ten and hardly anyone was at the beach since it was not officially summer. The Italians like their timetables and hardly anyone goes to the beach before June or after September even though the weather is hot. Beach attendance has a set time. In the morning the old people come for the morning sun. At lunch they go home. In the afternoon the younger people come. The young men in their Speedos and the girls in bikinis coyly lie on their backs trying to keep their virginity intake for mama's sake. As I laid on the beach listening to music on my player I noticed a man staring at me. He was older, probably late forties, very thin and very tan. He looked remarkably like my old boyfriend from Monte Carlo. When I got up to go home he followed me down Lungomare Marconi, the street which runs in front of the Hotel du Bain along the sea. I stopped at the corner to wait for him. He invited me for a drink at the bar across the street.

He was an architect from Padua. Although he had his own business, he still lived with his parents. Was there any man in Italy who did not live with his parents? He was successful, nearly fifty and still living with mama.

It wouldn't bother me so much except for the need of these guys to call mama every day and report in. He did make a phone call to his mama to check in. The Italian mama thing is a phenomenon that produces extremely selfish and demanding men. What woman could possibly take her place? Big grown babies. But still he seemed interesting.

We agreed to meet the next day.

The next day we met and went to the beach in front of the cabanas of the Hotel du Bain. His name was Giuseppe, or Pepe. Pepe was a northern Italian. He was not tall, 5'6", with brownish hair slightly graying and very thin. He did his two hundred crunches every day to keep his stomach flat.

As I was lying on my stomach at the beach next to him, he started playing with my ass, running his finger up and down the crack of my ass. We were on a semi-crowded public beach and I was somewhat embarrassed by what he was doing so I buried my head in my arms. It was late May. The beach cabanas were not yet open but some men were working to get them ready for the opening next week. We took our towels and went in between two rows of cabanas. Except for the men working, we could enjoy some semi-privacy there. Italian men always allow a little freedom to their comrades. We were kissing hot and heavy when Pepe's hand slide inside my bathing suit bottoms even though there were people not twenty yards from us. It's amazing how passion can make you forget that other people are around. Finally, even the cabana worker could not tolerate our behavior any more. He told us to leave. Pepe and I walked down to the deserted bit of beach between the sea and the old veteran's hospital. We found a spot somewhat hidden by a sand dune and tall sea grass. My bathing suit bottoms were off in a minute (not that they provided that much protection), my legs were up in the air. Neither of us lasted too long. It was nearly six in the evening and the sun was already going down so we made plans to meet the next weekend.

# CHAPTER NINETEEN

**THE** next weekend I met Pepe at the Vaporetto on Lido and we took the bus to the southern end of Lido. There is a short street with some businesses, a park and a boat stop but we walked toward the beach--Alberoni. Almost at the beach, we took a trail that headed into a small forest of pine trees. Ten minutes into the forest we took another trail which led to the sand dunes. Several men, some of them naked were standing up with their hands covering their eyes from the sun. They were obviously looking around for something. At first I thought they were looking for ships. But they weren't looking at the sea, they were looking at the other dunes that separated the beach from the forest. Pepe told me this is where the gay guys come for some quickies. Suddenly I felt like I was in a Fellini film -- it was surreal but beautiful, the white sand against the blue sky and dark blue sea and the men standing naked on sand dunes.

I wondered why he had brought me here. Was he gay?

We soon found a little nook between the sand dunes. Pepe, with an efficiency that proved he must have done this before, sent up our little day camp. Two towels, water, tomatoes to eat like apples. Five minutes later we were naked. He took out his camera and started taking pictures of me. I gave way to the pleasure that was sweeping me in this strange open place. It was strange to be out in the middle of the sand dunes with a guy when I looked underneath my arms I saw someone else. There was a young guy, half hidden by a bush, who was watching us. I boldly looked at him, but I didn't say anything to Pepe. The boy didn't move when he saw I was looking at him. I watched this young boy as he stared at us as we fucked.

As the day went on and Pepe and I continued our sexual escapades, the young boy moved closer and closer to us until he sat only five feet from where we were. I thought that he was going to join us. I would have liked him to join us. Pepe and I stayed until the sun set without ever saying a word to the boy. We walked back to the little town and ate ice cream in the park. On the bus back to town I saw the boy who was watching us. I guess his day at the beach was over too. It was time for all of us to go home.

# CHAPTER TWENTY

PEPE had another adventure for me the next weekend. We walked through Lido toward the northern tip of the island. It is only a twenty minute walk past the hospital and a couple of cabanas towns. We took a trail through the sea grass near the small airport at the tip of the island. There we climbed to the roof of a World War II gunner shelter. It had a very flat roof which meant no one could see us, but we could see everyone. We laid our towels out on the roof and sunbathed naked. After an hour another couple climbed up to the roof. They said nothing to us or us to them but they laid their towels out on the hill about ten feet away from us. They took off their clothes. The man sat on the towel looking at us. The woman laid on her stomach and did not look at us.

"I licked her pussy last year," Pepe told me.

"What?" I asked.

"Last year, here on the beach, she was here with her husband. They are exhibitionists. They like people to watch. And they like to watch."

The woman was in her late 40's and neither skinny nor fat. She continued lying on her stomach and still didn't look at us. The man was good-looking with very strong muscular legs. He was looking at us intensely.

Pepe pushed my legs back while the man watched us. I guess I am a natural actress and being on this cement stage I started the performance. I watched the man the entire time. It's the eyes that connect people during sex. I was thinking Pepe had arranged all this with the couple, but the woman seemed not at all interested. After an hour of sex on the rock, I got tired of the whole thing. Was I ready to have sex with another couple? With this couple on this rock? Perhaps I would have if the woman had seemed interested. But she continued to ignore us. It seemed like such a big leap. I had often fantasized about having sex with a woman. It would be an experiment, I told myself. Something I should do to further my education. But now with a couple I didn't know, was I ready for that? Complete strangers having sex. I was turned on by the idea, but also turned off. It was a line I wasn't able to cross.

Suddenly I jumped up, grabbed my things and climbed down the rock. No, I wasn't ready. I wasn't going to do this with some Venetian couple. I could see them on the streets. Venice is a small town. As I quickly climbed down the rocks, Pepe followed me. He was still naked.

"What are you doing? Where are you going?" he yelled after me.

I had ruined his plans and he was more than angry. "Troja," was the last word I heard from him. "Slut".

No, I wasn't a slut. That's the whole point I thought to myself. I'm not a slut.

I quickly walked back to my home and took a bath.

What was my life becoming here? What was I becoming?

I had two lovers supporting me and fucking another guy and now I was suddenly into group sex?

I didn't hear from Pepe the next week. I continued my weekly Saturday nights with Andrea but I was becoming frustrated with that relationship. It was obvious that it was just sex to Andrea. I was convenient, willing to do anything and I had no Italian girl's expectations. He had his neat little life and I was just the Saturday night express fuck. He was becoming more distant. There were no more songs sung in bed. Maybe it was because my roommates were so much younger than me that he became aware how much older I was.

On Tuesday I went to Santa Margarita to meet my girlfriend students for a drink. Now that it was summer we liked to meet at one of the bars at seven for a drink and a chat. Santa Margarita is full of Venetians in the summer. It's close to the university and families and children stroll on the large square. San Marco is the famous tourist square in the city, but Santa Margarita is where the Venetians go in the evening. I looked up from our table and saw Andrea walking with a girl. A young girl. He didn't see me he was so intensely listening to this girl. I had never seen him outside our relationship. I realized how right it was for him to be with a twenty year old girl. I was too old for him, that's why our relationship was always hidden. He was the type of guy who would get married to some nice Venetian girl and have two children. Reality is sometimes heartbreaking.

Raphael and I continued to see each other but Raphael had no desire to have relationship. If he loved me or even liked me, it didn't matter. His life was scoring up as many girls as possible and adding to his list of conquests -- Jennifer from New York, Sybil from New Zealand, and Keiko from Japan -- they were names on his resume, his love resume. And could I blame him? It is easier to know many lovers and not feel too much for any of them. I had Andrea, Raphael and Pepe. Well, Pepe I wasn't so sure of anymore. He was pretty pissed at me after the rock incident. I needed a decent guy.

A few days later when I was on the vaporetto I saw a nice looking man. I realized it was the doctor who I met when I first week I came to Venice. Yes, that's what I needed -- a nice doctor. He didn't seem to notice me on the boat but a week later he called.

"Ciao, do you remember me. I'm Antonio," the caller said.

"Yes, I remember you," I said. "And yes I wanted to see you again".

Just when I need rescuing, the doctor comes to my rescue.

We met the next day for dinner at the vaporetto. He took me to his house for dinner, which he prepared in his precise, Italian way just as his mama had taught him.

Next we were on his sofa watching bad Russian porn. So much for nice doctors. He was just as horny as every other Italian. I wanted to be in love with him. That would have made my life so much easier. But when I went home I knew I would never love him. He called me persistently for the next month. At the end I just hung up on him every time.

Two weeks later Pepe called again. He suggested a two day trip to Croatia. I'd never been to Croatia, in fact I didn't know anything about the country. But he planned a weekend with us leaving the next Friday. Croatia sounded cool and Pepe was a lot of fun in bed. This was an experience I could handle.

# CHAPTER TWENTY-ONE

**FROM** Lido I took the vaporetto to the train station. A trip that takes more than an hour of floating through the lagoon and the Grand Canal. A cool breeze blew from the east and the morning was crisp and quiet without the rush of tourists even though it was the middle of June. The canal seemed dreamlike in the morning that day. I was lost as I watched the sun on the rippling waves. That morning I felt really alive. Like I was part of the world and the world lived in me. I arrived at the train station and took the train to Mestre. Pepe was waiting for me with his car. We drove to the auto route and made our way up the Italian coast to Trieste and crossed the border into Croatia. After a while on small mountain roads he found the major highway heading south. The strange thing about this highway was that it was new and there's no cars on it. We are alone on a perfectly new and grand highway, more like something you would see in the America with large wide lanes, not the narrow lane pay highways you generally see in Italy that are in need of repair. Then there is a sign that explained everything. "Built by the United States Army". Oh yes there was a war here and the Americans always like to build highways wherever they go. This comes from fact that Hitler realized he needed to get men and tanks quickly across the country so he started building highways across his country in the 1930s. After World War II the Americans started building the great grid of highways across and up and down America. The country became a country of highways which, of course, led to Americans using the highways which led to the massive consumption of oil which led to...well you know that story.

That's the best thing about America having a war in your country. The roads are bound to improve.

It's a five hour trip. By the early afternoon Pepe and I arrive in Rovinj. The Croatia coastline and her ports where once ruled by Venice for several hundred years and the port of Rovinj was built by Venetians as part of their empire. It was a strategic point for their trade to the east. The town embraces Venice's architecture combined with the easy, primitive style of Greece. It is a beautiful place with a small harbor and tiny stone houses on a little hill that make up the old town. Pepe and I walk through the streets looking at embroidered tablecloths and pottery. We arrived at the top of the hill with a church. There was a wedding with the happy bride and groom and parents holding their children. Everyone seemed happy at the wedding as if every day was filled with such joy and family values in this place. I felt that perhaps this is an omen for me. Perhaps I will finally get married. I saw three brides the first day I was in Italy and this surely must be a premonition that I was going to get married. And Pepe, he had all the criteria. He was an architect. He had money. He had his own house (even though he doesn't live in it). Think positive. He was educated. He was past wanting children. He was great in bed. I'm thinking like an American. Americans think of life as a list of things to do. Things to accomplish. Things to look for in a partner. There are books to read if you're not quite sure what you want. *"52 Ways To A Better Organism"*, *"Three Secrets To Losing Weight"*, *"Ten Things Women do Wrong"*. Well, that's just about everything I've done. But what they never include in the books is the wrong stuff is usually the fun stuff.

We ate by the sea. Right by the sea. I mean the waves were splashing on my feet. We walk back to the hotel. We fuck. I mean we came here to fuck. That's the main social activity and that's what we did. No dips in the hotel pool. No sunset walks by the sea. We stayed in our room and fucked for the rest of the day and night.

In the morning we went down to the dining room where a beautiful display of food was arranged in the large dining hall. This must be a hotel for the German tourists because there are omelets which are cooked to order, sliced hams and liverwurst, cheeses, bacon, muffins, cereals and coffee. Five large tables of goodies are laid out. Italians never eat big breakfasts. We loaded our plates with more food than we could eat all day. Pepe asked me to get him another cup of coffee. I jumped up and fetch him another cup. I am often obedient. Left over from my days with the Monte Carlo boyfriend/dictator.

We left by eight o'clock to go to a nudist camp near the town. It was my first encounter with a nudist camp. We parked and brought a day pass. It reminded me a little bit of Disney as we brought our ticket and entered through the gate. The only thing that was missing was a sign "Welcome to Naked World". Most of the people there were staying for a month and some people lived there all year long. There were hundreds of mobile homes with well-manicured lawns. I guess all that extra time you save not washing and ironing your clothes you can devote to the garden. We took off our clothes and walked in our tennis shoes through the streets. I tried to be nonchalant about the whole thing and walked casually as if I were just walking down any street. The first naked man I saw was mowing his lawn. People were sitting in lawn chairs talking with their neighbors. A man was watering the lawn and waved to us. It's a nice regular neighborhood only everyone was naked. Did I have a nightmare about this when I was a kid?

There was a large swimming pool area with a few children swimming. We walked down to the beach at the end of a little lagoon. The water was crystal blue and cold. We spent the morning swimming. Lying on the beach we watched a young couple playing in the water. Pepe and I left our little idealist naked world in the early afternoon to go back to Italy. The real world.

Our weekend was over and the five hour trip here was an eight hour return trip. The cars were piled up on the Italian side with a gridlock at the toll booths. Welcome back to Italy. Croatia seemed like a well-organized country, an Italy of forty years ago with not so many people or cars. Italians and their pay booths. I wish they'd get a clue.

# CHAPTER TWENTY-TWO

**ANOTHER** crisis came the end of June. I had the Lido apartment for only three months. On the first of July we were to be kicked out for the summer rentals. Madame Visioni had the same tenants every summer. One in July and another in August. The rent was six times what she charged during the rest of the year. And where was I to go now? Even with the money I had from Andrea and Raphael I had to find another apartment. A single room this time where Andrea and Raphael would be free to go anytime of the day or night. I dreaded looking again. It seems my whole life in Italy was looking for a place to live. Andrea found an apartment near the Ghetto. It was close to Andrea, about ten minutes from the station but on the other side of the city as far as

Raphael was concerned. It was a room in an apartment with a young man, a musician, and his even younger girlfriend. The only problem was it wouldn't be available until August. I had to find someplace to stay for a month. I decided to go to Lake Garda. I stayed at the hostel in Riva del Garda. I've stayed here before and it's the most perfect place in the world to me. The little town sits at the top of the lake and is guarded by two thousand feet cliffs of rock on the north side. By the lake there is a park and beach with docks in the cold clear water. The town next over is Torbole which is world famous for the wind surfing. Hundreds of wind surfers and sailboats glide across this ideal lake in the summer. For me it's a place of complete contentment. It's a good place to rest after my year with Andrea and Raphael and Pepe and Dario and ... well, you know the list goes on. But the problem was once you get a taste for men, they are like a drug and you can't stop. So I didn't stop. After a week in quiet Riva, I went straight forward to Florence.

While at Lake Garda, I made three internet connections. Two with men in Florence, the other a twenty-year-old boy from Hawaii who was staying with his cousins in Cinque Terre.

# CHAPTER TWENTY-THREE

**WHERE** to stay in Florence? That is always the big question for me. I've stayed in Florence a few times before at two different hostels and a convent but I wasn't really happy in any of those places so I looked for a new spot. Sven, a Swede, was living in Florence and he had been consistent with the emails and offered his place as a place to stay but I'm hesitant about staying with him.

What if I don't like him and I'm stuck there? Even though I don't have much money I opt to stay at the big villa hostel on the edge of town. I've tried to stay there before but it's always been busy. I take the bus out to the edge of Florence and pull my suitcase up the hill to what was once a beautiful villa that has been transformed into a hostel. All hostels are the same in that they're crazy and fun and this one is no difference. A beautiful room with twelve bunk beds and twenty-four girls. Maybe it's a man's dream to be stuck in one of these rooms with so many young girls, but as a woman, even a woman who likes girls, it has its limitations. I make plans to meet Sven in front of the Duomo at five o'clock.

At five I walked by the church and there he was, sitting on the steps smiling at me. With my finger I called him over to me. He followed me. We talked for a few moments then I got on his motorcycle with my short skirt trying not to show all of Florence my crotch. Visions of Britney Spears ran through my mind.

If nothing else came from this trip, riding on the back of a motorcycle through Florence with a man I barely knew made this trip worth it. It was such an Audrey Hepburn thing to do. He took me to his apartment which was only a few blocks from the hostel. It's small (apartments in Italy are either incredibly small or unbelievably big). A one room deal with a separate kitchen with a tiny one person balcony that held a few tomato plants. We immediately went to the sofa. No point in pretending I'm here for any other reason. Despite the fact that Sven was Swedish and a tour guide and was exposed to about a hundred girls a week he was pretty innocent when it came to sex. He married at a young age and most of his conquests have been young girls who don't know anything so with me he finds a teacher. We had sex a couple of times that night until it's time for me to go back to the hostel. I asked him if I could stay with him for a few days. The offer he gave me before I came was now withdrawn.

"No. I wouldn't feel comfortable with you staying here," he tells me.

OK, so I'm short of money I'll have to go down the list to the next guy.

# CHAPTER TWENTY-FOUR

**THE** next guy on the list was a lawyer and also offered me a place to stay. He also sounds sexually perverse so he sounds like a good candidate. I sent him an email that night when I got back to the hostel. He promptly replied in the morning and told me to come. I told him I was just arriving in Florence and would be at the station at eleven in the morning. He offered to meet me at the train station.

I waited nervously for him at the station. This was really crazy. He could be crazy. I must be crazy to go off in a car with a strange man. He could kill me. These thoughts buzzed through my mind when Matteo walked toward me. I knew it was him because he was the only man who was dressed like a lawyer at the train station. Lawyers, in general, do not take trains.

He kissed me on the lips like he's known me forever. He grabbed my bag and told me to follow him. Matteo was short, a bit stocky with the face of a Renaissance angel. He did not give me a chance to back out. He was as determined to win his case here as he must be in the courtroom.

He carried my suitcase up the four flights of stairs and asked me what I had in it. Again, a small apartment, one room and a kitchen. It didn't matter whether you're a tour guide or a lawyer, all apartments are small. He put my suitcase down and pushed me to the couch. OK, there's not even going to be two minutes of foreplay talk. No what would you like to do? No a few light kisses to warm up. His tongue was down my throat.

He pulled his cock out of his suit pants without even taking off his coat. He pushed his cock into my mouth while I'm thinking what I have gotten myself into.

"So what do you like?" he asked me after I sucked his cock for a few minutes.

A man who was so blunt deserves a blunt answer.

While the beginning might have been a little quick we fucked the rest of the afternoon. It was Friday and Matteo had no more appointments that day. Outside the bedroom, Matteo was a gentleman. He took me to a delicious restaurant in the hills overlooking the Tuscany countryside. No tourists here. We drink red wine from San Gimingnano, a small town not far from Florence which is known for its towers and its wine. I ate a steak, juicy and tender and delicious.

While at dinner Matteo suggests a plan for the weekend.

"How do you feel about a gang bang?" he asked me.

"A gang bang?" I answered.

How DO I feel about a gang bang? Well, I don't really know since I've never thought about it before. A gang. A gang of hoods, definitely not. A gang of good-looking guys all wanting to fuck me... well that was an ideal with potential.

"Mmm, I don't know. Maybe," I answered.

"Well, I have some friends and we sometimes get together with a girl and," he paused for a moment, "we all fuck her."

"Oh," I answer, "I don't think so."

It's not that I wouldn't like to be fucked by a couple of good-looking men at the same time but this sounds out of control. It's all really about control. Who's in control me or them? Me, good. Them, not good.

"Come on you'll like it," he said.

"No, sorry. Wrong girl."

"Well, I do have another friend. My best friend actually. We've been friends since we were children and he's never done anything like this but he wants to try it. Would you be interested in something with him?"

"I don't know, Matteo, really this is just a little too weird for me."

"He's the one who told me about your ad."

"What?"

"Yea, he saw your ad and emailed you a couple of times. He told me to check you out."

"And you did."

"And I did."

"What's his name?"

His name was Marco.

Yes, I remember Marco. I had sent him many emails and he sent me some really sweet ones back. I had always intended to see him when I was in Florence but all of the sudden he stopped emailing me.

"Marco, yes I know Marco," I said.

"So would you be interested in something with him?" Matteo asked.

Oh yes, I thought Marco was really hot -- a beautifully handsome yet pure man. Very Florence in his looks he had light brown hair and a handsome face, about 6'1" and by all indications in his emails a sweetheart.

"Perhaps," I answered.

Matteo was a good lawyer, very successful and I can see why. A good lawyer is a good salesman. He offered me a really big deal -- sex with many guys maybe five or six of them, then he made me a counteroffer -- sex with one other guy, a guy I had already been talking to and him. This was an offer I could accept.

I was seriously thinking about it. It could be fun. It would definitely be interesting. Plus he said the magic words which made me say yes.

"You will be the Queen. You will be the center of attention."

I'll be the Queen. The Queen. Ordering my servants around. Yea, it's good to be the Queen. OK, the Queen will do it.

Matteo called Marco and made plans for the next day. We would all go to Marco's aunt's apartment by the sea.

The next morning Matteo went to pick up Marco by his house. He was waiting for us at the corner and quickly jumped into the back seat. He was shy and hardly wanted to look at me much less talk to me.

"So what do you think?" Matteo asked Marco as though I wasn't even in the car. "She's hot, huh."

Marco gave me a quick look.

"Yea, just like Britney Spears."

As we drove out of town to the freeway I felt great. Really great. Two guys could be a great thing. A fantastic thing. How many times did I want to fuck my boyfriend's good-looking best friend? About 563 times. Being the center of attention between two guys was definitely a thing worth exploring.

We arrived at the apartment and I went immediately to the bedroom.

"I'd like to be alone with Marco first," I said to the two men. "You fucked me last night. Give Marco and me a chance to get to know each other.

"Ok," Matteo said not too pleased with the notion but Marco was his best friend. He was willing to make the sacrifice.

Marco had hardly said anything to me in the car but in the bedroom he went into immediate action. He pulled off my shirt and bra.

"My god you have the most beautiful breasts. Are they real?"

"Why don't you feel for yourself?"

He grab them hard then sucked my nipples while I arched my back.

"You like them, huh?" I asked.

"Oh yes."

"I like this," I said as I rubbed his hard cock with his pants on.

"Oh, fuck," he cried out.

I bent down and pulled his pants off and proceeded to give him a blow job.

"Ooo Dio," he cried out as my lips encircled the tip of his cock. "Braaavoooo oh."

Next he was on top of me, fucking me, kissing me.

"You are so hot," he said before he made the last hard thrusts into my pussy.

We were laughing, caressing each other when Matteo walked into the room.

"So was it good," he asked Marco.

"Yea."

Matteo who walked in with only his underwear on, quickly took those off.

He moved to the other side of me.

I was facing Marco kissing him while Matteo pressed his body against my ass and played with my tits. Matteo was hard and so was Marco despite the fact he had just come five minutes ago.

"Let's do a double," Matteo said.

Yea, let's do a double I thought. I'd seen this in porno films and I always wondered how a woman managed to have one cock in her pussy and another in her ass. Well I guess I was about to find out.

I got on top of Matteo and slipped his cock into my pussy. Marco kneeled behind me and pushed his cock into my ass.

There it was. I was doing it. One cock in my pussy and one in my ass. And it did feel great. I WAS THE QUEEN.

That night my two guys took me to dinner at a rustic old restaurant in the hills, another place only known to locals where we ate sausage and mushrooms and cheeses and ravioli and steak and bread and, of course, drank a lot of Tuscan red wine.

Afterwards we went back to the apartment and watched TV. While Matteo took a shower and Marco fucked me on the couch. I slept with Matteo in the big bed. Marco slept alone in the little bed in the other room.

I wanted Marco, but in the morning he was cold to me. In fact both men were rather cool. No more queen for me. The queen's reign was over. She was dethroned.

We took the car an hour south to a place full of people but not so full of beach. We perched ourselves along with a hundred other people on the rocks and tried to pretend we were comfortable. I moved close to Marco and kissed him on the neck.

He pushed me away and said, "We have the pope here you know."

We have the pope. What exactly does that mean? Ok, stay away from Marco he was obviously having some moral crisis over what happened last night. I guess it's tough to be a horny Italian.

For lunch we drove to San Gimignano. I was in the back seat this time. My status as Queen had definitely diminished. I had been demoted to the back seat like luggage. Marco and Matteo were talking like I was not even there. I was banished to the back seat and in solitary confinement for my sins of yesterday. What a harlot. With two men.

We drove through the middle of nowhere on roads where there were no other cars. I thought these guys could take me to a deserted part of the road and kill me. What's stopping them? Nobody knew I was with them. My writer's mind came up with an entire story. My death. Their disposal of my things. It would be so easy. And who would miss me. Well Raphael and Andrea might eventually notice I was gone.

Just when I had convinced myself that they were going to kill me, we pulled in the car park at the foot of San Gimignano. We ate pizza in town mostly in silence.

Back at Matteo's apartment, Marco went to the supermarket. I went to the internet place. I had to make plans for tomorrow. I stayed away a long time hoping to avoid Marco. The "we have the pope" comment got me mad. Well, if you have the pope you don't need my pussy. When I did come back to the apartment, Marco was gone.

I spent a restless night sleeping in the loft bed at Matteo's apartment while Matteo slept on the sofa. The next morning I took the bus back to the train station. Matteo didn't even offer to give me a ride. The queen's reign was really over I guess. But the queen was a survivor. I already made plans to meet a guy in Lavente, a town in Cinque Terre.

# CHAPTER TWENTY-FIVE

CINQUE Terre is only two hours by car from Florence but it took me six hours to make all the train transfers. Florence to Viareggio to La Spezia to Lavente. And of course the waiting in between. But I was excited. Fabio sent me a picture of him and although American, raised in Iowa and living in Hawaii, he looked totally Italian. He was staying with relatives in one of the small towns in Cinque Terre so with what really little money I had left I got a hotel room. He offered to pay for half of the hotel room. I asked him on the internet to get a hotel since he was already there but he couldn't because he didn't have a credit card. Well neither did I.

I got off at Lavente, a small beach town with two dozen little hotels. I walked to the first one I saw and asked for a double room. Eighty Euro. An extravagance for a woman with little money and no job but Fabio really looked good. In the room I called Fabio told him where I was staying. I took a bath and waited. Two hours later I heard a knock on my door. I opened it. Standing before me was a very tall (6'4) and very skinny man. Fabio was fabulous. A face which reminded me of Jesus Christ. I was attracted and at the same time repelled by him. He was too skinny, too young and too much like the naked Christ hanging on the cross. There are times with most online romances when you finally meet the guy and you think this was all wrong. This was not what I expected.

But he's here, the hotel was already paid for and I was horny. Although I just spent the weekend fucking two guys in Florence, I was still horny. Actually I'm on a roll. Sex is a lot like gambling, when your luck is up you go with the flow.

We got naked and got to it. But he really does look a lot like Jesus and I can't help thinking I was having sex with Jesus. This is really a bad thing to think if you were raised Catholic by nuns and I was. Also, he was so skinny, I feel like a tard of blubber on top of him. Sex is not good when it involves guilt or low self-esteem so I switch from my pleasure to his. At seven in the evening we are finished and he said he was hungry.

"I'll go get some pizza," he suggested.

"You want me to go with you," I answered.

"No, I'll just be gone a few minutes."

"Do you want a key?"

"No, I'll just knock. You'll be here won't you?" he asked me.

"Sure."

He left. I was so tired from the train trip, the anticipation, the waiting that I fell asleep. An hour later I woke up.

No Fabio. Fabio didn't come back. It can't take more than an hour to get a pizza. Slowing it dawned on me that I've been dropped. If he had to go why didn't he just tell me he was going? Why come up with the pizza story? Oh yes, he promised to pay for half of the room and now he doesn't have to. I could have called him but it's better to leave dead dogs lying. Lady luck has turned her back on me. Or so I think.

# CHAPTER TWENTY-SIX

THE next day I go back to Florence. Should I stay in the hostel again? Going back to Florence had no appeal for me. I decided to skip Florence and go to Roverto, a town north of Verona. There is a nice hostel there, quiet, and a single room with my own bath is only twenty Euro. I can mellow out for a while after by Florence trip. I arrived and got on the internet. There was an email from a man. This is what it says.....

Hi! First of all let me tell you that I got your picture and you look splendid! I found your ad very intriguing as you go straight to the point and seem to know exactly what you want. Good, I like that in a woman. I'm 44 years old. My compliments again, you are a beautiful woman!

My questions are: Where do you live? What brought you to Italy? What do you do and what are your plans now? What do you look for in a man?

I am Swiss-Italian (from Geneva) but have lived in the US for 13 years (San Francisco + L.A.). I am an independent financial advisor and I travel to Italy very often (on a weekly basis) as the majority of my clients are Italians. In the US I got my undergraduate and MBA, then worked for the large bank in San Francisco for a couple of years (i.e, I am financially "sound"). I eventually would not mind going back to live and work in the US (although not a must). As far as my looks, well, you won't be disappointed either. I'm 5'8", athletic, and in the US I took on a few modeling jobs in my spare time... I do not have many pictures of myself so for the occasion I took a quick shot with my cell phone (enclosed)...Sorry for the quality.....Let's talk! If you feel confident enough, give me a phone # can call you at, if not, still ok!

This man sounds perfect. Just what I'm looking for-- he was educated, had lived in the U.S. and was not twenty years old.

And a picture. I saw his face and thought this is a face I could love. I responded and Carlo said he could come to Verona to meet me the next day.

I took the morning train to Verona hoping to meet THE ONE.

Verona, the city of Romeo and Juliet. I love Verona. I've stayed there before and feel comfortable in the little town enveloped by the Adige River. Carlo said he would meet me at the café across from the amphitheater. It was two in the afternoon when I called him and told him which café I was at. He was just on his way to meet with a client but would meet me at the cafe after his meeting.

I waited. A half an hour later a man's voice from behind says "You're more beautiful than your picture."

I looked up. My heart was racing. This could be it. This could be the man. Every cell in my body was telling me this could be the man. He was attentive and interesting. After an ice cream he took me in his car to a hotel in the country. We were talking nonstop. There was no slack of conversation between us and he missed the exit to the hotel. Still we're talking, driving through the Italian country side.

He pulled into a small country inn. The back parking lot is full of Mercedes, Jacquards and a Maserati. In the room there was no awkward moment. We were naked and in bed in one minute. The attraction was everything. We were making love. Not just sexual acts. We were connecting. My feelings were so strong that I was scared. This man could change my life. I was already thinking of going to Geneva, of living with him after knowing him for only one hour.

We went downstairs at nine to eat dinner. Carlo had stayed at the hotel many times on his business trips and the owner knew him well. We were served a scrumptious meal. The meal was great but I hardly tasted anything I was so possessed by Carlo. We went back to bed and spent the night making love. I was so excited by this guy

I could not sleep. I rubbed his legs, cradled his head, and hugged his body.

The next day at breakfast he started to talk. He had an ex. An ex-girlfriend he still saw even though she had been living with another man for a year. She snuck off on the weekends to spend time with Carlo but they didn't have sex.

"I spend all day with her and go home by myself to jack off."

Hello, I thought to myself, here I am. Someone who's ready to love you. But he doesn't make love to me that morning. He was thinking about his ex. He felt guilty that he didn't call her that morning. He took me to the train station and we kissed goodbye.

"Let me know where you are going," he told me, "maybe I can meet you in Venice."

But I don't want to be part of a threesome again. His mind was still preoccupied by his ex-girlfriend and there was no room in his life for me.

Whatever I felt for this man, I had to run away from it. He left me stunned, unable to think. I ran back to Venice. I ran back to Raphael and Andrea. Raphael and Andrea I could handle.

# CHAPTER TWENTY-SEVEN

BACK in Venice it was still one week before I could move into my new room so I called Raphael to let him know I was back in town. I got a bed in the hostel at Santa Fosca. Raphael told me that one of his old American girlfriends was in town. At least I was being told about this girl, last year he just dropped me for a month.

I knew about Robin, she was probably Raphael's oldest girlfriend "who comes for visits". He has known her for six years and for five of those years she had a serious boyfriend in Los Angeles which was where she was from. Every year Raphael visited Robin and her boyfriend when he made his annual trip around the world to visit all of his girlfriends. They didn't have sex, but now Robin has broken up with her boyfriend and she's here in Venice for a week to visit Raphael. And I imagine the no sex thing was off.

Raphael suggested we meet for a drink together. He has a fantasy of getting me and Robin and him together in bed. Well you can't blame him for trying. I'm not at all keen on the idea. I knew Raphael fucked other women but I didn't particularly want to be there when he did it. I was jealous. There I admitted it. I told Raphael that I was exhausted, which I was. Just that morning I was leaving Carlo at the train station and my heart was exploding with feeling I didn't want to deal with.

"Maybe tomorrow," I told him but I was thinking about excuses to put it off for a while.

The next day Raphael called again. He suggested meeting him and Robin after work and then we'd all go to the beach. Well I'm bored. Pepe was in Padua all week and I wouldn't see Andrea until Saturday. And I need something to distract me from thinking about Carlo. I agreed and at five o'clock I crossed the bridge to Raphael's work. He was there in the large foyer, impeccably dressed in a lime green jacket and pressed white linen pants. With him was a beautiful dark-haired woman. She was dressed in a short skirt and a low cut blouse to show off her breast job. She paid a lot of money for them so she had every right to show them off. Actually I was happy with Robin's looks. She was the complete opposite of me so there was no direct competition. If she had been a skinny blonde I might have felt different.

We were coolly friendly with each other. She's had more experience meeting Raphael's girlfriends. She's met two or three of Raphael's girlfriends in the U.S., but no ménage came from it. We both knew what Raphael wanted and we both were avoiding any conversation which might lead to his desire coming true.

We are, after all, both American women and American women are predatory about our sexual partners. As pretty and sexy as she was I had no intention of having sex with her and Rafael. He can have sex with her if he wanted but I was going to make a retreat before it happened.

We had drinks on the lounge chairs at the beach and then went back to the cabana to change. In the shower I avoided Robin and when she changed into her street clothes in the cabana I left. She, I was pretty sure, felt the same way that I did, so we were both working in conjunction to foil Raphael's plans.

We had dinner together at Lido and then took the vaporetto back to San Zaccaria. We stopped at Chioggia bar, the bar where Raphael's brother worked. Raphael's brother and another waiter fluttered around us and brought us glasses of Prosecco. Raphael was beaming as all his competitors in the square saw him with two hot chicks, both of whom he was known to have sex with.

After our initial hesitation Robin and I became easy friends. We shared more than Raphael, we shared being women. And that really was the only binding we needed. We had experienced the same disappointments and the same desires in life.

Robin and I were opposites. She was a tall, stately with dark hair and large breasts. They were fake boobs, but they were impressive and actually seemed to fit her body as if she should have been born with them. She was a Sophia Loren type -- more standoffish than I. I started to call her Sophia and sometimes Lucy (I was Marilyn or Ethel). But I admit it, Robin was hot.

I was blond, slender and smiling all the time. I was always happy and ready for some new adventure. I sometimes took Robin along for the ride. Surprisingly, the jealousy between us diminished, maybe it didn't disappear altogether, but we could confide in each other. It actually turned out really nice 'to share'. Neither of us were in love with Raphael and that's probably why we got along. We were just along for the fun ride.

Raphael saw that Robin and I were getting along and around ten o'clock Raphael suggested that we ALL go back to Robin's apartment. I quickly backed out. I liked Robin, but I still wasn't ready to cross that fence.

"So sorry, I'm so tired. It was nice meeting you Robin, I hope you have a great time here," I quickly added before I turned and walk off. Raphael yelled something after me but I hurried down the street below the bell tower.

Raphael called me the next day.

"So did you and Robin have a good time," I asked him.

"I just took her back to her apartment and went home," he answered.

"No sex?" I asked.

"No, she's on her period. Besides I was tired."

Oh good, I thought. Even though I knew Raphael screwed a lot of other women, I was happy he didn't screw this one.

"Do you want to have dinner tonight?" he asked me.

"What about Robin?"

"I don't know. She's always a nuisance. I think I'll just tell her she's got to do something on her own. Besides I haven't been with you for a couple of weeks. I want to fuck you."

I was appeased. I was the winner. I was willing to do what he wanted.

"Ok," I said and made plans to meet him in San Bartholomew Square at six.

"I don't feel like going to the beach, "he told me on the phone. "Let's stay in town tonight."

As I walked toward San Bartholomew square I could see that Raphael was not alone. No, there was Robin. I greeted both of them with kisses on their cheeks but I was pissed.

"Let's go to the Monaco and Grand Canal Hotel for a drink," Raphael suggested.

The bar at hotel overlooks the Grand Canal and the Salute church. It's one of the best and most intimate bars in Venice. It was past seven by the time we got there after stopping in San Marco to talk to one of Raphael's many friends.

The sun was just beginning to set and about ten pairs of ballroom dancers were dancing on the steps of the Salute church. It was an enchanting site and Robin and I both started to loosen up. We girls began to talk. We talked as if Raphael wasn't there.

"You know what Raphael wants," I said to Robin.

"Yes, well a guy is allowed to dream, isn't he," she said.

"Yes, Venice is a place for dreams. It's meant for dreams, isn't it," I said and then looked over at the dancers as they gracefully moved to the music which was playing at the bar. We had no idea what music they were actually dancing to because they were too far away. The sun was dropping below the island of Guidecca and Raphael ordered second glass of Bellini for both Robin and myself. Robin and I were both loose when we left the bar.

On the way out Raphael saw his friend Paulo who worked at the front desk. Robin had met Paulo at the beach several years ago where they had a long discussion and some mild flirting. Paulo who immediately recognized Robin was ready to continue his seduction of her and completely ignored me. He probably would have come with us except that he had to work. So Raphael, Robin and I left the bar.

When I asked where we were going to eat, Raphael said, "at Robin's apartment. I bought everything already ... some beautiful melon and prosciutto, some lovely cheese, pasta with asparagus and wine. And bread, of course." Raphael's father had been a baker and Raphael used to work in his father's bakery when he was a teenager.

This wasn't what I agreed to in the morning on the phone but I was hungry and to back out ... well I was too jealous of Robin flirting with Paulo that I had to assert some female power.

The apartment Robin was staying in was in fact Raphael's brother's apartment, an apartment he shared with another guy and an apartment I had no knowledge of before this night.

I had had a lot of problems finding a new apartment in Venice and in fact had to go to Lake Guarda for a month until the apartment I finally did find was ready. But Raphael never offered this apartment to me, but Robin had it for the whole week.

I quietly simmered with anger while Raphael prepared our dinner. I was so angry that I went down stairs to have a cigarette and I nearly walked back home without saying anything, but again I was jealous of Robin and didn't want her to win the night. She had already won the apartment.

I went back upstairs and I was willing to fight.

As I walked up the stairs it's as though I was going on a stage. I left my body and another character assumed my body. As myself I would do nothing. Too many years of Catholic training would keep me from going any further. But as someone else I could do anything. We had dinner and I was delightfully charming to both Raphael and Robin. I complimented Robin on her body, her hair, and her clothes. After dinner we pulled out the sofa. It was decided I would spend the night and sleep on the sofa. We watched a little porno movie. I was on the sofa with Raphael, Robin was sitting in a chair.

"Would you like a massage" I asked Raphael.

"Yes," he said taking off his clothes and lying on his back. I took off my dress and sat naked on Raphael ass and rubbed his back.

"That's a nice site," Robin said to us.

"Come here and join us," he said to Robin.

"No, I'll just watch you two."

Raphael turned around and I sat on his cock and started fucking him.

"That looks good," Robin said.

I got off and started sucking Raphael's cock.

"Come here Robin. Suck me too," Raphael said.

To my surprise Robin came over and we took turns sucking Raphael's cock. It was interesting watching another woman suck cock. I watched her technique. I learned from her.

"Do you want your pussy licked?" Raphael asked Robin.

"No," she said, "I'm on my period."

"I'll lick you," I said. "I'll just stick your little string in your pussy and no one will know."

She opened her legs and I started licking her pussy. She was shaved clean and she barely had a clit or pussy lips. Her skin was smooth and soft and I liked running my tongue around her pussy. I had had a dream about it when I was about twenty and I was shocked that I would even think about such a thing. But it had remained a secret fantasy of mine for all these years and now I was doing it. Well it was a night for fantasies and I completed a few more.

When we finished Robin went to bed in the bedroom and Raphael and I fell asleep on the sofa. In the morning we all got up. Raphael went to work and I kissed Robin on the cheek and walked with Raphael to his work.

The next couple of days I saw Raphael and Robin at the beach but when we went back to Venice I didn't go back to her apartment with them. I needed time to adjust. Raphael wasn't my boyfriend, but in a way he was. I was screwing Andrea and Pepe so how could I feel hurt by his being with Robin. Robin was here for only a month. Then she'd be gone. I would have Raphael back in the end. But there were many things that made me sore. Raphael's mother was in the hospital and it was Robin he took to see her. It's true that Robin knew no one else in the city and she depended on Raphael for everything so when he had to visit his mother naturally she would come along. I lived here. I had other friends, had classes to teach, I wasn't with Raphael all day. In fact I usually just saw him three or four times a week. I had my other guys. But I was still sore about his dropping me for a month while another girl visited town last summer. That anniversary was about to come along with another birthday.

Another birthday. Fuck. That was really depressing me. Another birthday, another year older. And Raphael was planning on taking Robin to a hotel near Lake Garda for a night. It was my birthday and he was taking her somewhere. This was not going where I wanted it to go. The character I had assumed that night was gone. I was back. And I was unhappy. Somehow, by mentioning it was my birthday in a few days, I got asked along for the night out to Lake Garda. So the three of us left Thursday afternoon at two in the afternoon after Raphael got off work. Robin and I met at Piazza Roma with our little suitcases and waited for Raphael. We had to take the bus to get to Raphael's car which he kept in Mestre. About three o'clock in the afternoon we finally set off in Raphael's twenty year old red Toyota to Lake Garda.

Lake Garda is one of my favorite places and I was sitting in the front seat with Raphael so I was somewhat appeased as we drove east to the lake. As nice as Robin and I were with each other, there was always the undertow of competition. She had known Raphael longer, so she thought her relationship took precedence. I, however, was the girl he spent the last year with, so I thought I took precedence just by the amount of time I had spent with Raphael. If you added up all the days Robin had spent with Raphael in the last five years it wouldn't have added to two month.

We found the hotel, an old hotel set in a park in a small village about five miles from the lake. We were waiting on the bench when the owner came to us to register us. She asked our names.

Raphael gave the lady his full name, Robin's full name but with me he just said my first name.

"What's your last name?" he turned around and asked me.

We had been going out for a year and he didn't even know my last name. It dawned on me how little I meant to him.

Our room was small with a little kitchen but the bathroom was enormous. And in the middle of the bathroom was a hot tub that could fit ten people and a platform in the middle. These Italian apparently knew how to have fun.

It was nearly seven-thirty by the time we got into the room and we all were ready to find a place to eat. It was a little conclave of buildings, not even a town, and there was only one restaurant. We went in. There was a large party of fifty people in the main hall. There was only one table left outside in the back and we filed past the private party made up of mostly Italian men in their thirties. Need I tell you they were horny Italian men (are there any other kind) and the presence of Robin and I caused a minor hooting and hollering riot.

We sat at our little table and Raphael ordered the dinner. We had only gotten a few sticks of bread after a half an hour wait when it started to rain. I don't mean a nice little sprinkling, but a full blown thunderstorm from the Alps.

We ran inside the restaurant. Of course they had no place to put us. After waiting another half an hour I went back to our room telling Raphael to call me when our table was ready.

Needless to say, I wasn't having a good time. I laid on the bed thinking of a way out. I needed to think of a way out of this situation. Maybe I was interested in fucking with another woman. And Robin certainly was attractive, but unfortunately Raphael was making me feel used. I felt like nothing. I was an afterthought to him. I wasn't even a real person with a real last name.

Raphael called. I went to the restaurant and we had a quick meal as our table was now by the front door and I spent most of the meal moving my chair for the customers leaving to get out the door.

The three of us walked back to the hotel. I knew what was expected of me. I had done it a few night before and I would have to do it again. So the character, the wild slut character, took over again.

We all went into the hot tub. Robin and I were both shy at first. Despite our competition, we both felt for each other. And we, in our way, looked out for each other.

"Why don't you eat her pussy," Robin suggested to Raphael.

He did. I responded. A few minutes later Robin was lying on her stomach on the platform in the middle of the hot tub. Later in the bed I watched while Raphael fucked Robin's ass. Raphael and I slept on the bed together. Robin had wanted to sleep alone on the sofa bed.

The next day we went to a water spa with a cave. We three swam together while everyone watched us. I stood next to Robin rubbing her back while she came on the water spout.

Robin was only staying for a month, when she left my life could get back to normal. Normal being alternate days with Raphael, Andrea and Pepe. And no competition.

Back in Venice for one day, Pepe called me. He invited me on a four day trip to Croatia for my birthday.

# CHAPTER TWENTY-EIGHT

PEPE wanted to leave at eleven o'clock at night. I met him at the train station in Mestre. We drove the six hours up the Italian coast to Croatia and down the empty highway toward Split. I slept. It was early morning when we arrived and we stopped for breakfast and gas. By eight we had arrived to take the ferry across to the island Hvar.

Like Rovinj, Hvar used to be Venetian territory, an outpost for ships heading to Cyprus and Turkey. Our destination of the little island of Palmizana which was now, at the height of summer, filled with tourists. Pepe found a bed and breakfast, an apartment house with four floors. An old lady, her forty-something daughter and her twenty-something granddaughter lived on the first floor. The second floor were their bedrooms and the top two floors had four bedrooms for guests. Our room was small but decorated with modern furniture and mirrors against the wall in back of the bed. Since it was still morning Pepe and I walked down to the dock where we could catch a small motor boat for a smaller island fifteen minutes away. This was our real destination, another nudist colony. We walked ten minutes past the rocky beaches filled with tourists with bathing suits on until we reached a fence. A man who sat on a stool collected our fee to the nudist camp. It was a day camp, unlike the previous nudist colony which was full of long-term campers. We took off our clothes then walked down the dirt path along the rocky shoreline. This camp was full of people. Families with their children, single men roaming around. On an outcrop of rock several couples had their towels and lounge chairs out for a day in the sun. We took a place between two young couples. We swam in the cool aqua blue waters and later went up to the restaurant for lunch. A sign at the entrance of the restaurant requested that everyone wear clothing while eating. I guess there are times when you just don't want to see someone's balls or other things. I ordered Werner Snichel, Pepe ordered pasta. In the afternoon we went for a walk in the woods which was part of the park. By five we headed back to our room. We had romantic dinner in small restaurant courtyard in a garden surrounded by stone walls.

# CHAPTER TWENTY-NINE

**THE** next day was not as pleasant as the first. Pepe and I were a good couple together because we didn't spend that much time together. Now after about thirty-two hours together we were getting bored. We went back to the Nudist came. But Pepe was no longer interested in me. He ogled the other women. He openly stared at them. Perhaps he was trying to get something going with one of them so we could have a group thing. But his staring only made me mad. I had been with a threesome with Raphael and Robin and also with the two lawyers from Florence, why was I so hesitating about doing something with Pepe and someone else.

A threesome is tricky work for a man. You must not pay too much attention to one woman over another. You have to treat them both like gold, because at any minute one of them could feel hurt, humiliated, jealous or just not in the mood. This was Pepe's mistake ... he ignored me.

That night we went out to dinner at a café outside of town. Pepe ordered our meal and two glasses of wine. Pepe asked the waiter for a second glass of wine for himself.

"I'd like another glass too," I said.

"No, one glass in enough for you."

WHAT! What did he just say to me? I didn't know what to say. Was he really telling me I couldn't have another glass of wine because ... I couldn't think of a valid reason?

I didn't say anything. In fact I didn't say anything else all night. The mood had changed and it was only on the way home he asked me what the problem was.

"The wine. You told me I couldn't have another glass of wine," I said.

"Yes. You only need one glass," he replied sternly.

"What do you mean I only need one glass? Who are you to tell me what I want or what I don't want."

We went back to the hotel. No fucking. When he turned over to pull me to him I said in English, "I don't think so."

I never spoke English with Pepe. I don't know if he understood me (I doubt he did) but he understood the meaning.

The next morning, Sunday, we had breakfast in silence.

We were supposed to stay until Tuesday, but Pepe proposed we leave that day and I agreed. I was determined to end it with him but I had to get home. I was in Croatia with no money. I needed Pepe to get home so I kept all the words I wanted to yell out in my mouth. We quickly packed our things and told our surprised hostess we were leaving early.

Driving the car in silence we were hardly out of town when the traffic in front of us stopped. It was the last Sunday of the Italian vacation period. All of Italy takes their vacation at the same time, the first two weeks of August, and we along with thousands of our compatriots were headed back to Italy. We were stopped at this road because we needed to take the ferry back to the mainland. There is no bridge off the island. After an hour of creeping along in the car I got out to walk and see how many cars were in front of us. Two hours later and 567 cars later we boarded the ferry to the mainland.

If our mood was not good beforehand this only added to our anger. When he stopped for petrol about five hours into our trip I considered trying to find a ride with someone else. I practiced my speech in my head "Hi, I'm stuck here. Can you give me a ride to Italy?"

To make matters worse what little money I brought with me was gone. I had no money. I was starving.

"I'm hungry," I told Pepe.

"Well, I'm not going to fucking feed you. Starve, you little whore."

I was inside out with anger, but I keep my mouth shut.

The rest of the ride was a nightmare. Traffic was stopped all along the way. Finally when we seemed so close to Venice, about fifty miles away, we got caught in the biggest traffic jam at the toll booth. Five hours we crept along. When we made it through I suggested to Pepe he drop me off at Quartino de Alto. I could take the train home and he could take the back roads to Padua. He agreed. And with no goodbyes we said goodbye.

# CHAPTER THIRTY

I returned to Venice and my first day back Robin and I met at the beach while Raphael was at work. We were confidants now. All the jealousy and competition was gone and we were becoming great friends. We could talk about anything to each other. I told her everything. We talked all day and when Raphael came we were still talking to each other and ignoring him. Not that we both didn't still adore him, we did, but in fact we had a lot more to talk about with each other than with him.

Robin was bored with Venice and I suggested a trip south to Brindisi. I had been in contact with a man on the internet who said he had a house by the sea.

"Just imagine it, a beautiful house above the stony cliffs of the Adriatic, " I told Robin trying to entice her into coming with me.

"Are there cliffs there?" Robin asked.

"I don't know. I've never been but if this guy wants to put up with us for a few nights, why not take the opportunity?"

"But what if this guy is a creep?" she asks me.

"If he is, he is. We'll go find a hotel for the night and come back the next day. But it could be fun," I tell her. "And I've never been to the southeast coast of Italy. I'd really like to go."

Robin, despite being a highly paid executive in Los Angeles, was a bit scared of going out on her own. She had come back to Venice six times in the last eight years but she never went anywhere else in Italy. As much as I love Venice, all of Italy is such a beautiful and exciting place. So finally I talked Robin into joining me for a few days.

The trip To Brindisi from Venice was neither short nor exciting. We took the day train, a train that goes slowly down the coast, one seaside town after another. We arrived at the station and got off the train. Robin and I together looked a little like Sophia Loren and Marilyn Monroe getting off the train in our tight day dresses. We were both a lot of curves and bosoms. A man ran towards us. It was Stephan, a man from Ireland who was obviously overjoyed at his catch. Did he bring in two big ones! My previous conversations with Stephan indicated that I was going to have sex with him, but that I was bringing my friend who was not going to have sex with him. But men are men and they do dream.

Even though it was six at night, the first order of the day was for Stephan to take us to the local hangout, like every other Italian town, the café. Here he paraded us around, and the way he walked around with Robin and I on each arm it was a parade. We, of course, knew our roles, roles we have played with Raphael so many times that we took it in stride. Of course any guy was going to be so pleased with himself by showing off two gorgeous girls to his friends.

We were anxious to see his house by the sea. Well, it was neither a house nor by the sea. A small apartment in the middle of town, about five miles from the sea, we looked around the little living room and I saw Robin was ready to bail out. But she was a good girl and kept her cool. Stephan meanwhile was doing everything he could to make both of us perfectly happy. He produced a bottle of wine and trays of cheeses and pastries. We were tired so it was better here than out of the street with no place to stay for the night.

He put on music and Robins swirled around the room with her white skirt floating. So we're not staying at the Ritz, but still this could be fun.

Stephan was not at all my type at all. He looked much better in his photo than in person, but he was an interesting man and I realized a deal was a deal and I had sex with him. Robin came up stairs to the bedroom with us. While Stephan ate my pussy, Robin was sitting next to me reading the local tourist guide. I moaned under Stephan's tongue.

When he went to the bathroom Robin said to me, "He must have been good. You were really moaning."

"No, I was just acting."

"Wow, you're pretty good at that."

"Lots of practice, darling, lots of practice."

Around nine in the evening, Stephan took us to a local party up in the hills. There was food, wine and music supplied by the town council. About fifty people showed up and we were the topic du jour. Two American girls with the Irishman. Stephan lived in town full time and knew everyone in town. I danced with Stephan and then Robin danced with Stephan.

When we went home Robin slept in the living room on the sofa. Stephan and I went upstairs to sleep in his bed but I said I was drunk and hot and wanted to sleep on the roof. He came up after me and tried to have sex with me on the roof, but I feign sleeping and he left me alone.

The next day Stephan took us to the beach. He positioned himself in between Robin and myself. Having had me and after Robin told him she wasn't interested in him, he goes after Robin all morning. He ignored me and turned his full attention to Robin. He caressed her back, her thighs, kissed her fingers. I was happy, at least he was off of me. Perhaps Robin will grow to like him. But she declined his persistent offers.

In the afternoon, we head to Trulli, the quaint little town of Trulli houses, houses made to look like cones and look like something that trolls should live in. The entire town is composed of these adorable little houses and we walked through the town and ate gelato.

Stephan was consistently pursuing Robin but she wasn't biting. I went up on the roof when we got home to let the two of them talk. Perhaps with me out of the way something could happen... but two hours later Stephan came sniffing around me. I turned over and told him I had my period.

"Sorry," I said.

It was a complete lie.

But really if he thought he can pay attention to Robin all day and then when she wasn't interested, come back to me, well, do I have to say it, he had another thing coming.

The next morning we went to the café for coffee. We were a big hit with a group of older men who wanted a picture of the both of us sitting on their laps. An old man put his hand on my boobs but it was all in good fun. Robin and I laughed at our popularity, this town hadn't seen so much action since ... OK it's probably never seen this much action.

Stephan took us to another beach. His pursuit of Robin increased until she was slapping his hand off her legs.

Finally I said to him, "She's not interested in you, Stephan. Can't you get that through your thick head?"

I guess I really insulted him.

"You're just a jealous bitch," he said to me.

"If you only knew how completely not jealous I was," I countered.

"All you Americans think alike," he said.

Ok, now he got me mad. Americans -- we are the world's problem or so Stephan seemed to think.

"What do you mean all Americans think alike? We are a country of three hundred million people, all from different racial backgrounds, and yet we all think alike?" I yelled at him.

Robin stood back in amazement. She had never seen me mad. I stood up and pointed my finger at this guy. I can dish my country but if someone else does...

"Yea, all Americans think alike," he repeated his statement.

"Really, and do all Irishmen think alike?" I asked him.

"No, of course not."

"So you're telling me that four million Irishmen who live on an island and come from the same genetic background don't think alike but that three hundred million Americans, more than a hundred times more, who comes from all over the world, from all sorts of ethnic backgrounds, think alike."

He couldn't win the argument logically, but that didn't stop him from continuing the argument. I yelled until the other beachgoers looked at us in amazement. So much for showing off his two women. I stormed off for a walk and came back an hour later.

It was cold between Stephan and me for the rest of the day and Robin and I decided to take the night train back to Venice. Stephan took us back to his apartment, we packed our suitcases and he took us to dinner -- a pizza. At the train station I walked to the platform without ever saying another word to him. Robin shook his hand goodbye. We waited for the night train which would take us back up the Italian east coast and back to our beloved Venice.

# CHAPTER THIRTY-ONE

**DESPITE** or maybe because of my angry repartee with Stephan, Robin and I had a fun trip back north. I loved riding the train at night. I had a bottle of wine and two glasses. The first hour we were alone, each of us stretched out on the three seats. An hour later four students joined us, our compartment was full with six people. Robin and I slept with my head on her feet and vice versa.

At six I woke up just in time for us to get off the train in Bologna to make our connection to Florence. We grabbed out suitcases from the overhead compartments and ran through the station to jump on our nearly missed train. We had decided to spend a night or two in Florence. I had told Robin about Sven and what a great guy he was. We could stay at the hostel for a night and take a look around Florence. I was thinking of calling Marco for a hook up. I still had bad feelings about leaving him and wanted some more time with him. And after seeing Marco's picture, Robin was interested in meeting him too.

We arrived in Florence at eight in the morning. I took Robin to the hostel in the villa. It was cheap but Robin had never stayed in a hostel before. Robin was a highly polished professional woman from America. And highly polished professional women do not stay in hostels. I told her it would be fun, it would be an experience and she hesitantly went with me. But she definitely had her doubts. Together we dragged our suitcases up the hill. It was nine in the morning when we got there. They wouldn't give us a bed until after twelve. We sat for an hour and Robin started to chicken out. She was just not the hostel type.

"Do you want me to call Sven?" I asked her.

I was trying to avoid taking Robin to Sven's. Her presence had caused a problem between me and the Irishman. If I had gone alone to see the Irishman there probably wouldn't have been the big fight. But, Robin was unhappy to be staying at the hostel. I called Sven and of course he was HAPPY to have Robin and I stay with him. (Now it was ok for me to stay with him now that I had a girlfriend with me when a few weeks before it wasn't ok for me to stay when I was alone. Men.)

We went to Sven's apartment. Seeing a picture of Sven before we went she said that he wasn't her type and she didn't want to have sex with him. OK. Once in the apartment Robin said she wanted to go shopping in Florence and she would be back in the evening. Sven and I spent the afternoon fucking.

With Robin back at the apartment at six o'clock, Sven began to make a beautiful meal. Fresh tomatoes from the plant on his balcony, eggplants and artichokes from the market. We all sat in the kitchen drinking wine. After dinner, our conversation turned to sex.

"So you're not interested in having a threesome?" Sven asked Robin point blank.

Robin looked at me as if to say, oh no not another one.

"No, I'm just not in the mood," she said sweetly to him.

But Sven was charming and educated and an hour later Robin agreed to both of us giving him a blow job.

"Just a blow job, nothing else," Robin told him.

"Just that would be great," Sven said grinning as wide as his mouth would allow.

Two minutes later Sven was stripped and Robin and I are going at another cock together. Sven was very happy -- he took a picture of his little blond and little brunette. That night I slept with Sven and Robin slept on the couch.

The next day Robin and I headed back to Venice.

# CHAPTER THIRTY-TWO

AFTER our trip south Robin was still antsy and went to Verona for a few days. When I met Raphael after work he said his friend Lorenzo had a girlfriend in town and she was... amazingly... bisexual. She was from Paris. Raphael and Lorenzo had visions of a great big orgy. Raphael had to sweeten me up first and took me for a drink at the hotel Europa & Regina on the Grand Canal. He had made plans for Lorenzo and his date would meet us there, but they never came. On the way back to my apartment, Lorenzo called. He and Rebecca were on their way back to his apartment. Would we like to meet? I hesitated. I was tired, it was late and there's always an emotional price to pay with a threesome, now this would be a foursome. Just what was I becoming? I guess I was now a certifiable slut (remember Single Lady Under Transition.)

"Let's just meet them and you can see what you think?" Raphael said to me.

"Ok," I didn't want to be rude but I was expecting I wouldn't like her.

Fifteen minutes later we met them on the street. This was the first time I had ever met Lorenzo although I had seen him in the square many times. He had tried to pick me up several times but I had always said no. Even though I was tired, my interest peeked the moment I saw Rebecca. She was a petite brunette with a pretty face. Her family had come from South America but she had lived in Paris for the past fifteen years. We didn't speak with each other but to our respective mates. We both said yes.

The four of us went to Lorenzo's apartment. Unlike most of the men in Venice, Lorenzo had his own apartment.

"His father has money and bought it for him," Raphael told me.

Unlike most of the other Venetian apartments I saw in Venice, Lorenzo's apartment was beautifully furnished with modern sofa, glass dining room table and several art pieces. Lorenzo, Rebecca and I sat on the sofa while Raphael remained standing. Perhaps Raphael was shy being with another man but he just watched while Lorenzo and I unbuttoned Rebecca's dress. Her breasts were small and round and as I caressed them. Lorenzo and I each took a breast sucking on them while our hands caressed her body. Her dress was off. Then her panties. Faced with an audience the actress comes out in me. Watching porno does pay off.

We were all kissing when Raphael came over and kissed Rebecca. Rebecca and I were naked but the boys were still dressed. We all went to the bedroom and everyone was naked. We switched partners. Lorenzo was fucking my pussy dogging style while Raphael was fucking Rebecca's pussy with her legs up in the air. Lorenzo finished quickly. He got up to get a camera and took pictures of Raphael, Rebecca and myself going at it. In ten minutes Raphael was finished but Rebecca and I were still hot. The boys left us alone in the bedroom (maybe thinking it's all over since they've had their orgasms) but Rebecca and I stayed in bed kissing.

We heard the boys in the living room talking about sports.

"They don't know what they're missing," I said.

I finished Rebecca off before the guys noticed what we were doing. It was late. Raphael and I said goodbye to our hosts. Raphael walked me back to my room and left me alone at my apartment as he usually does to go back to his mama.

# CHAPTER THIRTY-THREE

**THE** next day I went to visit Andrea at his shop. He closes at one o'clock for the afternoon lunch break so I came ten minutes early and waited in the back room for him. At one o'clock exactly he pulled down the metal covers to the windows and locked the door. He fucked me on the table in the back storage room, on a piece of newspaper. His touch was sweet and tender as always, but something was missing. Was he getting tired of me? I thought about him and the young girl in Santa Margarita Square. She was a better age for him. Someday he would marry a girl like that. He would never marry me. I mean I would never marry him. But still I wanted him and I wanted him to want me passionately again. So after sex when he was in a hurry to leave to eat lunch with his family I said, "I have a secret. I sometimes sleep with other girls."

He turned around quickly. Lunch was no longer on his mind.

"I love your secret. It is always my dream to be with two girls."

Yeah, what a surprise.

"Well, maybe I could make your dream come true," I said.

"O Dio, yes. You can?" he said before he kissed me.

"Yes, well I have a girlfriend in town. I sleep with her sometimes and maybe she will do this if I ask her."

I was thinking of Robin. She was coming back from Verona tomorrow. Of course I had been with Robin with Raphael and with Sven in Florence but with Andrea that was another matter. I loved Andrea and I didn't really want to share him with anyone else. Andrea was my boy love, my sweet love. Could I do this for him? It would be only for him, for his sake. For me, it would kill me. But he had been a good lover to me this past year. He helped support me and I should do whatever I can to make him happy. Even if it was bound to make me unhappy.

The next day when Robin came back to town, she and I went to the beach as usual and waited for Raphael to get off of work.

"Robin, I have something to ask you."

"Oh, no. I can just guess what it is," she said.

"Well you know about Andrea. How beautiful he is. What a great lover he is. He wants to make love to two women. I wonder if you would mind being that other woman."

"I don't know. You and your guys. They all want to have sex with two girls. It's not really something I'm interested in."

"Yes, I know, but Andrea is different. He's not like other guys. And he's gorgeous. And he's so sweet. He is a total joy to make love with."

I showed her a picture of Andrea. It was one he gave me when he went to Greece one summer. He was six-pack heaven.

"Oh my god," Robin said, "he is gorgeous."

"And so nice, and such a good lover, gentle and caring."

I really didn't need to go on, Robin was sold with the photo.

So I arranged for the three of us to meet at Robin's apartment the next afternoon.

At three o'clock I went to meet Andrea at San Lio square. From there I would take him back to Robin's apartment.

He came up behind me and tapped my shoulder. We walked side by side through the maze of streets.

"So how do you feel?" I asked him.

"Nervous. Excited but nervous."

"Me too," I said.

Was I doing the right thing? It was too late to back out now.

We walked to the apartment where Robin was waiting for us in her black bra and underwear. She wore fishnet stockings I had given her to wear. She was standing up.

"This is Robin," I said to Andrea.

"Very nice, very nice," he said in his accented English.

He kissed me and walked over and kissed her. He took off his shirt. Andrea is an Apollo. Really a perfect stomach with a neatly defined six-pack. I'm sorry Brad Pitt but his stomach is better than yours. 4% body fat.

"You like?" he asked Robin.

"Yes," she laughed.

Andrea took off his pants. There was no stopping this guy. He was ready to go. Robin sat on the couch and Andrea sat next to her. I knelt on the ground in front of both of them. He kissed Robin and then me. Andrea must have watched a lot of porno because he was doing it like a pro.

After a few minutes of Andrea moaning, caressing Robin's black hair with one hand and my blond hair with the other hand, we all went to the bed.

After a little rest we started again but a phone call interrupted us. Robin jumped up to get the phone. She was nervous when she came back to the bedroom a minute later.

"Raphael's on his way over now. He'll be here in a few minutes," she told us. She was running around picking up her clothes and throwing our clothes at us.

"I'm sorry Andrea, you need to leave. It's Robin's boyfriend," I said to Andrea.

Neither Robin nor I wanted Raphael to know we were screwing Andrea. I don't know why we cared, Raphael had paraded other girls in front of us for years. So what if we had a little fun on our own. But perhaps it was better this way, Andrea having to leave so quickly. He was out of the door before my remorse crept in.

As Andrea walked down the stairs from my apartment I sat down on the stoop and felt like crying. Never fall in love with a man younger than you. Never fall in love with anyone I thought to myself. I was only convenient sex for Andrea. I would never be anything else. How could I be so stupid? And I had always played a little bit of the innocent with Andrea hoping that one day he would feel the same way about me that I felt about him. But I could forget that now. Now I really was a whore bringing him other women to fuck. I only did it because I felt his interest in me was slipping and I had to do something to keep him attached to me.

Andrea, before he turned the corner, looked back at me. He was so happy. I smiled. I was so miserable. He had just fulfilled his dream of fucking two women at once. I smiled at him, for him. I knew how happy I had made him. It was a dream he never thought would come true. Bless his heart. For all his life Andrea would have this one day to remember. When he is an old man still working at the family store, he will tell his friends about his afternoon with the two American women. Of course his friends won't believe him.

A few minutes later Raphael showed up. It was very likely that Andrea and Raphael had crossed each other in the street. One never knowing who the other one was. Raphael took us to the bar. He and his two girls. Now he was happy. To make a man happy a woman has to sacrifice herself, her feelings. Raphael was happy standing between Robin and myself at the bar. He had a smug look on his face, a smug look because all his friends know he has slept with these two women.

Robin and I looked at each other and smiled at our secret. It was our café, or rather Raphael's café that became ours. We knew all the waiters and they all knew us. Or rather they knew all about us. Raphael was famous now. His legend confirmed by the presence of two women, one of each arm. Every man in that bar wanted to be Raphael. And every experience he had with Robin and myself was told, no doubt, to everyone and by everyone to their friends. This is the stuff that legends are made from. Raphael wanted to be a legend. He had come far from his days as an insecure teenager with a broken heart.

"My Sharona" was playing on the CD in the bar and Robin and I started singing with the song. We were both in high spirits after our two hours with Andrea. He proved to be the perfect lover I told Robin he was. That night we all went back to Robin's apartment. And in the same bed that Robin and I fucked Andrea, we now fucked Raphael.

Two days later Robin went back America.

# CHAPTER THIRTY-FOUR

I knew my time in Venice was over. All that I could do I had done. I could give nothing else to Andrea. I had given him the best present ever. After two women he would never be happy with me alone. And Raphael had never loved me, never cared for me other than the thrill I gave him of making his legend as a Casanova come true.

Was I happy when I lived there? Can a woman be happy without a husband and children and a home? Some women can. I was beyond happy. But other times I wallowed in despair, in unfulfilled love. I had lived a life, an exotic life, a life in a foreign country, in a beautiful city, I wore beautiful clothes and beautiful shoes and diamonds rings & bracelets. I had sexual encounters beyond my wildest dreams and I had a few moments of tenderness and love. I had known three wonderful men and lots of not so wonderful men. Because there were three of them I was never bored, sexually or otherwise. No matter how great sex was with Andrea and how much I loved him I knew if we had gotten married it would all get boring after a while. Sex with the same man or woman after two years can be boring. I'm sorry but this is a fact of nature. The human being was designed to copulate with many partners – it mixes up the gene pool. Men want to fuck every woman they see who is capable of producing a baby. Biologically that is what he is meant to do. Bees and flowers, baby, it's all just bees and flowers. Now women are in a more difficult position in nature. First of all they are the choosers. They are looking for good genes. And once they chose a mate, they want that mate to stick around. He needs to protect her and to hunt for her while she's in the delicate state of being pregnant and raising a small child. Let's face it, anyone who has been pregnant or knows someone who was pregnant knows that in the last month of pregnancy the woman is not going to be able to outrun the dinosaur. She needs help. She needs protection.

The male, apparently, realizes this and does try to hang around, but he's still looking. I could protect a bunch of these women he is thinking. I'll just keep them together in a little circle for variety. Oh yea, variety is good.

So I'm was bucking the system, the system which had worked for male-female relations for thousands of years. I'm the new woman, the woman of the twenty-first century who keeps several men and who keeps younger men. The only women who acted like this before where queens like Catherine the Great. Why not? Is it illegal to have sex with several younger men?

Did I love my life in Venice? Yes, although just a few years ago I would not even have thought such a life was possible. When I was younger I wanted one man. My one true love. But now I had many loves. Yes, I loved them all. They were each different and each complimented a different part of my personality.

But something drove me away from Venice and this life style. Perhaps my conscience, perhaps boredom, perhaps just the need to move on to something else. The next step. Actually the reason I moved back to America was money. I had no more savings. I needed to make a living again.

I love my life because I can't wait to find out what's going to happen in the next chapter. Life can be like that -- just like some great book when you can't wait to get to the next chapter and see what happens and then you are totally surprised by what does happen. So after two years of living in Venice, I left.

Now I'm starting a new story in my life. I just got married to a French man and we are living to Hawaii. But that's another story.

# ABOUT THE AUTHOR

**BLUE** Lynn Blake has lived all over the world, including four years in Venice and Assisi, Italy, two years in Monte Carlo on the French Riviera. She has also lived in England and South Korea. For fifteen years she lived in Santa Barbara and Los Angeles, California, and also spent many years in Minnesota and Florida. She currently lives on the island of Maui in Hawaii.

Printed in the United States
By Bookmasters